"You no-good, despicable—"

Her words were all-American, and his reaction was all male. There was only one way to silence her an he took it, lifting her to him and capturing he   with hi She struggled. She fought. He kep   ing h   way to k   er qu

T   self t   vning in he ste, h

"Do   ight me," he whispered against her lips.

one amazing moment she obeyed. Her   ftened; he let go of her fists and gathered her   is arms, bringing her tightly against him. Hei   s softened, too, and parted just enough so he c   d slip the tip of his tongue into her mouth and   or its sweetness.

until he felt the sharp bite of her teeth.

rsed, jerked back, and dragged his hand-ke   from his pocket. He put it against his lip, looked   the tiny crimson smear on the creamy white linen—and laughed.

Layla stared at him in disbelief. She'd bitten him and he'd laughed? Maybe she was losing her mind

THE SHEIKH TYCOONS

by
Sandra Marton

*They're powerful, passionate—
and as sexy as sin!*

Three desert princes—
how will they tame their feisty brides?

THE SHEIKH'S DEFIANT BRIDE
August 2008

THE SHEIKH'S WAYWARD WIFE
December 2008

THE SHEIKH'S REBELLIOUS MISTRESS
March 2009

THE SHEIKH'S
WAYWARD WIFE

BY
SANDRA MARTON

MILLS & BOON
Pure reading pleasure™

First published in Great Britain 2008
Harlequin Mills & Boon Limited,
Eton House, 18-24 Paradise Road, Richmond, Surrey TW9 1SR

© Sandra Myles 2008

ISBN: 978 0 263 86483 0

Set in Times Roman 10½ on 12¼ pt
01-1208-46198

Printed and bound in Spain
by Litografia Rosés, S.A., Barcelona

THE SHEIKH'S
WAYWARD WIFE

CHAPTER ONE

HE STOOD on a terrace outside the Grand Ballroom, looking over the deserted beach and the sea. A crescent moon hung in the sky, a cool ivory scimitar against the fiery backdrop of stars.

The pleasant sounds of conversation and music drifted through the partially opened doors behind him but he was alone.

Alone and annoyed.

The night was soft, the view enchanting, but Khalil had come to Al Ankhara on business, not in search of pleasure. So far no business had taken place.

He was familiar with everything here. The great Moorish palace. The white sand. The endless sea. He had been born here, not just in Al Ankhara but in the palace itself, born to all it represented. Legend said his nation was as ancient as the sea, as timeless as the desert. Once it had been a country of warriors. Now it was struggling to find itself in a new and different world.

Khalil was a part of both worlds. His heart would always be here, in this harsh and beautiful land, but his life was in New York City where he had lived for the past decade.

A frown crossed his ruggedly handsome face.

He had arrived early this morning, summoned by his father on what the older man had called an urgent matter of state. The summons had come at an inconvenient time but Khalil, although not a believer in some of the old ways, *did* believe in showing respect to one's father.

That his father was also the sultan gave the summons added weight.

He'd read the e-mail, cursed softly, then phoned to arrange for his private jet, leaving a billion-dollar deal on the table and a new mistress alone in her bed. Hours later he'd stepped off the plane, ready for anything....

And instead been greeted as if his homecoming was nothing but a usual visit.

Sheikh Khalil al Kadar, Crown Prince of Al Ankhara, Protector of his People, Heir to the Throne of the Lion and the Sword and, for all he knew, possessor of a dozen other outmoded titles, tucked his hands in the pockets of his trousers and sighed in frustration.

His father, surrounded by the usual coterie of ministers, had greeted him warmly.

"Excellent, my son," he'd said. "You wasted no time in getting here."

"Of course not, Father," Khalil had replied. "Your message spoke of urgency."

"It did, yes." One of the ministers moved closer and whispered to the sultan, who nodded, then clapped Khalil on the shoulder. "Right now, however, I have business to attend to."

"But this urgent matter...?"

"In a little while," the sultan had said, and hurried off.

The "little while" had gone from minutes to hours and as it did, Khalil's attitude had gone from curiosity to impatience to glowering irritation. His mood had not been improved when his father's private secretary had knocked at the door of his rooms in late afternoon to inform him that the sultan would see him at the state dinner scheduled for the evening.

Just thinking about it now made a muscle knot in Khalil's jaw.

How "urgent" could a thing be, if it was to be discussed while two hundred guests milled about?

Khalil had done his best to be pleasant during the meal, but he'd felt his temper rising. Finally he'd excused himself and come out on the terrace where he could pace its length, check his watch, wonder what in hell was going on and—

What was that?

A figure stepped from the shadow of the palace and began walking quickly along the beach toward the sea. Khalil frowned. Who could it be? The hour was late. More to the point, the area was private, restricted for the use of the sultan's household, and securely guarded.

One of the guests? No. The figure wore a hooded *djellebah*. A man's garment. But the men here tonight were all wearing dark dinner suits.

Khalil moved closer to the railing.

Besides, this couldn't be a man. The figure was too slight. A boy, then. A servant—but surely they would know that the sultan, a believer in the old ways, would not approve of a servant taking a stroll on this bit of royal land.

The boy had reached the place at which sea and sand met. Khalil's eyes narrowed. Was he imagining that there was tension visible in the line of the child's shoulders, the rigidity of his spine?

The boy took a step forward. The sea foamed around

his ankles. Around his legs, soaking the *djellebah,* wrapping it around them.

What the hell was the kid up to?

It was a fool's question. The boy was walking steadily into the sea—a sea that dropped sharply only twenty feet from shore and was often home to hungry, man-eating sharks.

Khalil cursed, grabbed the railing and vaulted onto the sand.

Layla's heart had been beating so hard as she slipped out the door of the harem that she'd been sure everyone could hear it.

She was amazed she'd gotten this far.

She'd slipped away without any of her guards noticing. Not that they called themselves guards. The two women who never let her out of their sight were her servants, according to her father, and when she'd glared at him and demanded to know what was the function of her third "servant," an enormous thug with a pockmarked face and missing teeth, he'd said that Ahmet was for her protection.

"Al Ankhara may look like a land of fantasy," he'd said, "but it is not."

That, at least, was true. Al Ankhara might look like something out of the Arabian Nights, with its minarets and Moorish arches, but it wasn't. What had happened to her in the past few days proved it.

But she had not let herself think about that tonight.

Instead, she had concentrated on escaping. The question was, how?

She and her so-called servants were in a separate part of the palace. It must have been beautiful once. Now the marble floors were dulled by age, the silk carpets were threadbare and the walls were grimy. The windows, looking out on an empty stretch of beach, were barred with decorative ironwork. The door that led into the palace was securely bolted; the lock on the door that gave onto the beach looked as if it hadn't been opened in the last century.

In other words, Layla was trapped.

Then, just before sunset, her luck changed.

A ship appeared. A yacht, if you wanted to be specific. It anchored off the beach. Two hundred, three hundred yards, maybe further out than that, but what did such a distance mean to a woman who was desperate?

How could she get to it? Not twenty minutes later, she had the answer.

She found a hairpin.

It wasn't the kind of little thing sold in drugstores. This pin was enormous, made of brass or copper. Or gold, for all she knew. What mattered was its size, its strength...

And that she could use it to jimmy the lock on the outside door as soon as her captors settled in for the night. Watching all those old movies about plucky heroines turning hatpins into tools might end up being the best thing she'd ever done.

She tucked the hairpin into a crack in the wall and waited.

The women brought her a plate of food, then waddled off to join Ahmet. Layla pushed the food around but didn't eat it. Soon, the women returned. She let them draw her a bath, let them dry her and powder her, but when they reached for a nightgown, she shook her head and mimed that she was cold.

The women snorted with laughter. Well, why not? Everything about her amused them. Her blond hair. Her blue eyes. Her pale skin and bony—in their eyes—body. That she should feel chilly when the temperature was probably just a few degrees short of spontaneous combustion was just one more thing that made them guffaw.

Instead of the gown, they'd dressed her in a *djellebah*.

"You sleep now," one had commanded, and Layla had dutifully gone to the alcove they'd designated as hers.

She'd waited until she heard a chorus of earth-shattering snores. Then she'd tiptoed to the locked door.

Minutes later, after some adept hairpin jiggling in the lock, Layla was free.

She'd wanted to race down to the sea, but what if someone was looking out the windows of the palace? She had to look casual, so she'd walked slowly along the sand. When she reached the water, she'd debated shucking off the *djellebah,* reminded herself she had no way of knowing who she'd find on that boat, still rocking gently at anchor. She'd just started into the water—

Something barreled into her.

Something big. Something powerful.

A man.

Strong arms closed around her from behind. Lifted her off her feet. She cried out, as much with fury as with fear. How could Ahmet have caught her this quickly?

Except, it wasn't Ahmet.

The feel of the body pressed to hers was hard and lean, not layered with fat. The arms encircling her were taut with muscle. Even the man's smell was not Ahmet's. Her horrible guard stunk of sweat and grease. The man who'd hoisted her in the air, who was grunting as she fought him, smelled of nothing but the sea and a hint of expensive cologne.

She was not going to be handed over to a fat bandit seeking a wife, Layla thought in disbelief, she was going to be raped by a hard-bodied, clean-smelling stranger!

Then she stopped thinking and screamed.

* * *

The scream damn near pierced Khalil's eardrums.

A woman? The creature fighting him like a wild thing wasn't a boy; it was a woman.

Very much a woman.

Holding her this way, tilted back against his body, there was no doubt about her sex. The hood of the *djellebah* had fallen back; her wild, silken hair was in his face, her backside was in his groin, her breasts...

Her breasts were damn near cupped in his hands.

By Ishtar, what was going on?

He was sure of only one thing. This was not the time to try and find out. She was doing her best to get loose. Well, fine. He would let her go as soon as she stopped trying to kill him. Okay, maybe that was an exaggeration, but her elbows were sharp as she slammed them into his gut, her heels were tattooing against his shins...

And that backside.

Small. Firm. Elegant. She was grinding it into his groin and, damn it, his perfidious body was starting to react.

"Bass," he snarled. *"Bass!"*

He might as well have said "stop" to a tiger. Khalil grunted, jerked her harder against him and put his mouth to her ear. *"Shismak!"* he demanded.

She didn't answer, but then, who would respond to such a question at a moment like this? Still, it was logical to ask who she was, what was her name.

Never mind.

What mattered was that they were still dancing in the surf, she fighting like a wildcat, he trying to subdue her...

Trying not to react to the bump of her backside, the fullness of her breasts...

Had he lost his mind? Who cared about any of that? The woman was an intruder. What was she doing here? How had she made her way past the gates and the guards? Had she come for a midnight swim? Was she trying to kill herself?

Footsteps were pounding along the sand. Khalil looked back, saw two heavyset women and an enormous man lumbering toward them.

The man had a blade in his hand.

"Drop it," Khalil snarled in Arabic.

The man skidded to a stop, stared, turned pale and fell to his knees. So did the women.

For a moment, no one moved, not even the woman in his arms. Good, Khalil thought grimly, and he spun her toward him, then dropped her onto her feet.

Hands on his hips, he let loose a string of words Layla couldn't possibly understand. She couldn't understand *any* of this. Why were her captors lying facedown in the sand, prostrating themselves before the madman who'd attacked her?

Gasping for breath, she tossed her wet hair back from her face and dredged up two of the three insults she knew. Well, she knew how to say them, if not what they meant, but what did that matter at a moment like this?

"Ibn Al-Himar," she panted. *"Inta khaywan!"*

One of the women gave a muffled shriek; the other one groaned. Ahmet rose to his knees, but the man who'd attacked her held up one hand.

He used the other to grab her by the wrist and wrench her arm behind her back.

"Shismak," he barked, lowering his face until his eyes were almost level with hers.

What did that mean? She was almost out of Arabic. The best she could do was lift her chin and toss out the one final insult in her pathetic vocabulary.

"Shismak," she said through her teeth and added, for good measure, *"Yakhreb beytak!"*

Whatever she'd just said, it certainly did the job.

He stared at her as if she were crazy. The women covered their faces with their hands. Ahmet shot to his feet and reached for her.

The man snarled at him and he fell back.

Silence descended on the little group, broken only by the hiss of the sea. Her attacker tightened his grasp on her wrist and dragged her arm high enough so the breath rushed from her lungs.

Maybe he wasn't going to rape her after all, Layla thought with amazing calm.

Maybe he was just going to kill her.

Enough. She had lived in fear the past few days, but she would not die in it. Instead she raised her chin and repeated whatever it was she'd said. Slowly this time, for the best possible effect.

Then she flashed a brilliant smile.

The man's eyes narrowed. *"Kelbeh,"* he growled. Then he put his big hand in the center of her chest and pushed.

Layla yelped, windmilled her arms and went down on her backside in the surf.

His audience guffawed.

He didn't. He went on looking at her, face expressionless. She struggled to her feet, shivering with rage, with fear, with her dousing in the sea, but her eyes never left his.

The man snapped out what was obviously an order. The laughter stopped. He spoke again; the women and Ahmet stood. They looked at each other, then one woman pointed at Layla and began speaking in a low voice. The man interrupted; the woman nodded. There was more pointing, more talk.

When it ended, the man swung around, folded his arms and studied her.

For the first time she noticed what he looked like. Tall. Broad-shouldered. Long-legged. He wore a black dinner suit, not a *djellebah*. His hair was thick and dark. She couldn't tell the color of his eyes but they were deep-set in a face that was harsh and hard...

And beautiful. Savagely beautiful, if there were such a thing.

Slowly, so slowly that she felt the deliberateness of it, his eyes moved over her. Over her face, her breasts, her body. She knew her soaked *djellebah* was clinging to her.

What could he see?

Everything, she thought. The shape of her breasts. The sudden tightening of her nipples. The length of her legs.

Layla made a little sound in the back of her throat. His eyes rose to hers. To her horror, she felt a rush of heat at what she saw in that beautiful, terrifying face.

The sound of the sea, the sigh of the breeze...everything faded. His lips curved in a smile, the kind that women always understood. Back home she knew exactly how to handle smiles like that.

Here all she could think of was taking a quick step back.

It didn't matter.

He caught her by the shoulders and tugged her forward. She stumbled, fell against him, against that hard, muscled body, her breasts soft against his chest. One of his hands traced the line of her spine; he cupped her bottom, lifted her into him and she felt the shocking power of his aroused flesh press into the vee of her thighs.

She gasped. Felt herself sway in his embrace.

He said something in a low voice. She didn't understand the words but the meaning was clear, especially when he lowered his head, threaded his fingers in her hair, tugged her head back until her face was raised to his.

"Balashs."

"Don't." She'd intended to say it forcefully, not in a tremulous whisper, but the way he was looking at her, the feel of his hand in her hair, the scent of him coupled with the scent of the sea…

Layla's heart pounded.

They stared into each other's eyes for what seemed an eternity. Then a muscle knotted in his jaw. He let go of her, shrugged off his dinner jacket and wrapped it around her. She clutched it without thinking, burrowed into its warmth, into the warmth that had been his. His hands closed on her shoulders again and he propelled her forward, into the outstretched arms of one of the women.

Then he turned his back, walked slowly up the beach and disappeared into the night.

CHAPTER TWO

KHALIL made his way to a little-used back entry to the palace he'd discovered as a boy.

It had been one way to avoid the rigid rules of behavior by which a prince was expected to live.

When he opened the door, a surprised royal guard snapped a quick salute; Khalil returned it without pausing and hurried up the stairs. He had no intention of returning to the ballroom. He hadn't been in the mood for all the glitter and noise earlier; he certainly didn't feel any different about it now.

What had happened on the beach was unsettling. Had he stumbled across something no one was supposed to see?

On the other hand, he thought, as he entered the sitting room of the suite that had been his since childhood, the scene by the sea had been played out with a lot of drama.

Who wouldn't have found it unsettling?

His shoes squished as he crossed the ancient silk carpet and went into the bedroom. He was soaked. His shoes, his trousers…

But that was what happened when a man held a wet woman in his arms.

A wet, all-but-naked woman.

Khalil paused as he stripped off his clothes. Definitely naked, under that *djellebah.* He'd always thought of a *djellebah* as a utilitarian garment.

Not anymore.

The soaked cotton had molded itself to her body, accentuating every curve. The roundness of her breasts. The feminine vee at the apex of her thighs, the delicate bud of her nipples pushing against the wet fabric....

His sex stirred and hardened. He shut his eyes, let his mind go back to those moments when he'd brought her against him, felt the softness of her...

Damn it!

Angrily he finished undressing, dumped his things on a chair and went into the bathroom.

He had reacted to her. So what? Any man would. There were far bigger issues involved here. Who was she? Why had she been on the beach alone? Why had she walked, fully gowned, into the sea?

Scowling, he stepped into the glass-enclosed steam shower and turned it on.

Her attendants said she was the daughter of a wealthy merchant, on her way to her wedding. She'd decided to take a swim even though they'd advised against it.

Yes, but they'd come running after her as if she'd slipped away from them. Why would she have to do that? She was their mistress. If she wanted to swim, she would. She didn't need their approval. They would have accompanied her to the water, the women tsk-tsking, the fat thug to stand guard, but they'd have had no choice but to accept her actions.

And why go into the sea wearing the *djellebah?* The woman surely would have known the wet weight of the gown would make swimming difficult.

Khalil bowed his head, flattened his palms against the glass wall and let the spray beat down on his shoulders and neck.

He should have asked the woman instead of her attendants. She had not said much to him, just enough so he'd noticed she had an accent he couldn't quite identify—and enough to rain insults on his head. She'd called him a donkey, an ass, a dog…

And he'd let her get away with it.

He'd let her stop him from kissing her, too, with that softly whispered, "Don't."

Not that he really would have kissed her. She was on her way to her wedding. That meant she was another man's property. Not that he believed in that kind of thing. Women weren't property. Not in his world, at any rate…

And why in hell would he have wanted to kiss her in the first place?

Better still, why was he wasting time thinking about a woman he would never see again?

Khalil shut off the shower, wrapped a towel around his hips, walked into the bedroom—and jerked back as the light came on and a spindly old man rose from a rug by the fireplace.

"Damn it," Khalil said sharply. "Hassan! What are you doing here?"

"Waiting for you, my lord."

"That's ridiculous! How many times must I tell you I don't want you waiting up for me, waiting *on* me…" The expression on Hassan's face stopped him in midsentence. His voice gentled. "Go to bed, old man. I can manage on my own."

"It is not proper, Prince Khalil. I am your servant. I should assist you."

"I am a grown man. I don't need assistance."

"You are a prince, sir. I was given to you at your birth. Tradition says—"

"Tradition says it is late," Khalil said gruffly. He slung his arm around the old man's shoulders and walked him through the suite to the door. "Thank you for waiting, but I can manage."

The old man sighed, bowed so low Khalil feared he might topple over, then backed from the room.

Tradition, indeed, Khalil thought as he closed the door. Would his people ever find their way into the twenty-first century, burdened with so many useless customs? He had grown up with those customs; he had followed them, as was expected, but more than a decade of living in the West had convinced him that some things had to be changed.

He dropped the towel, pulled on a pair of gray sweatpants.

The status of servants, to begin with. The veneration of royalty. The blind rigidity of law as dictated by the sultan, the crown prince...

Or a woman's father.

Khalil tumbled onto the bed, stacked his hands beneath his head and stared up at the coffered ceiling.

Something was wrong with the story he'd been told on the beach. Weddings practices in particular were steeped in tradition, but there'd been nothing traditional about the arrangements pertaining to this one.

When her people explained that the woman was on her way to be married, that she was the daughter of a rich merchant marrying an important chieftain, why hadn't he thought to ask the obvious questions?

Who was she marrying? And why was she traveling with such a small bridal party?

Two women. One guard. The details didn't add up. A wedding between people of wealth and power was an important event and surely this was such a wedding. Every possible honor would be given the bride. She'd be accompanied by at least a dozen horsemen. Easily that many female attendants. Members of her family, of her village.

And what of his father's role? Why hadn't he invited the wedding party to attend the elaborate dinner still going on in the ballroom?

Khalil rose from the bed, walked to the window and looked out.

The beach was deserted. There was nothing to show a woman had walked into the sea, that he had gone after her, that he had held her in his arms, felt the warmth of her body, smelled the freshness of her skin.

He might have imagined it all—but he hadn't.

Something strange had happened tonight. He knew that. He also knew it had nothing to do with him. This was Al Ankhara, an ancient place that held mysteries even he could not always understand.

Khalil went back to the bed.

One thing was certain. The incident had revealed a basic need. A need for a woman.

He'd ended an affair almost two months ago. He had a new mistress but he'd only been with her once before he'd flown here. Surely, that was the reason, the only reason, he'd been stirred by the woman on the beach.

He was hungry, and his hunger would be assuaged as soon as he was back in New York. The woman he'd left there had beauty and sophistication. She would greet him eagerly, wearing something sexy she'd picked up at Saks or Bendel's.

What man in his right mind would choose a fire-breathing female in a *djellebah* over that?

Still, when he closed his eyes, the face he saw was not that of his mistress but of the woman on the beach.

All the more reason, he thought as he drifted off to sleep, to find out what his father wanted of him, do it and return to New York as quickly as possible.

His father sent word they would breakfast together in a small courtyard centered on a fountain.

He was already there when Khalil arrived, seated at a marble-topped table set for two that was laden with platters of fruit, cheese, yogurt and freshly baked bread.

The sultan half rose; the men exchanged a quick embrace.

"*Sabah ala-kheir,* my son."

"Good morning, Father."

"Did you sleep well?"

"Very well, thank you."

"Please, sit down. Fill your plate. You must be hungry. You didn't eat very much last night."

Khalil looked up. The sultan's expression was innocent. The comment was not. What his father meant was that he'd noticed Khalil had not stayed for the entire meal.

"Was the food not to your liking?"

Two could play at this game. "It was excellent, Father, but I was weary from my journey."

Meaning, he had come a long distance on short notice and still had no idea why.

Father and son smiled at each other. They had not spent a lot of time together when Khalil was small—it was not the custom—but they had grown closer when Khalil reached adulthood.

"And how was that journey, my son?"

"It was fine. The skies were clear all the way."

"And your new plane?"

"It is fine, too, Father," Khalil said, trying to keep the edge from his voice.

"But what would truly be fine," the sultan said, raising his bushy white eyebrows, "is discovering why I called you home."

So much for word games. "Yes," Khalil said bluntly, "that would be a good thing."

Two servants hovered near a rolling cart covered with silver chafing dishes; another stood ready to pour coffee and tea. The sultan blotted his mouth with his napkin, tossed it on the table and rose to his feet.

"Walk with me, Khalil. Let me show you how beautiful my roses are this year."

What was this? Was his father concerned about being overheard? Khalil pushed back his chair and fell in beside the older man. They set off on a path of crushed white and pink marble that wound through the palace's fabled gardens.

When they were deep within its confines, surrounded by flowers and shrubs and far from anyone who might hear them, the sultan sat down on a wrought-iron bench. Khalil took the bench opposite his and waited.

"You were not happy that I requested your return," the sultan said.

"I was in the midst of an important negotiation."

His father nodded. "Still you came."

"You are my father, and you are the leader of our people."

The older man nodded again. "And you are my heir, Khalil. Since birth, you have known it is your duty to do what is best for your country."

What was happening here? Khalil folded his arms. "That is a given, Father."

There were a few seconds of silence. Then the sultan put his hands on his thighs and leaned forward.

"Last night, on the beach, you met a woman."

Was nothing about his life here private? It was one of the things Khalil had always disliked. Everything he did was subject to scrutiny.

"And?"

"She is called Layla."

Layla. A soft, feminine name. It suited her. The lushness of her body, the beauty of her face…but it was a direct contradiction to the fire of her temperament.

"Khalil?"

Khalil cleared his throat. "Sorry. I was… What about her?"

"She is to be married."

"So her people told me."

"It is an important union. Her father is Sheikh Omar al Assad."

"Are you certain? Her people said—"

"I am quite certain, Khalil. And her betrothed is Butrus al Ali."

Khalil blinked in surprise. "The renegade?"

"Not after this marriage takes place. Butrus will swear his allegiance to me, as will Omar, for brokering the union. An old and dangerous rift will be healed and our people in the north will finally have peace."

Khalil nodded. A marriage would take place for reasons of state. It was an old custom, not just here but in many parts of the world, and though he knew Westerners would scoff if he said such arrangements still took place among them, too, it was true; the sons and daughters of wealthy, powerful families often married to secure alliances and create dynasties.

But the woman on the beach, the bride of Butrus? He had met the man years ago. Could he recall what he looked like?

His jaw tightened. Yes, he damned well could.

Overweight. Hell, that was too polite a term. Butrus al Ali was grossly obese. He had long, greasy hair; there'd been caked black dirt under his fingernails and a stench to his breath that made it impossible to stand close.

The woman on the beach—Layla—was to take such a pig as her bridegroom?

"Khalil?"

"Yes, Father."

"Have you been listening to me?"

"I've been trying to remember the renegade. What I've come up with is not pleasant. The woman. Layla. Is she aware of his, ah, his shortcomings?"

The sultan cocked his head. "Should she be?" he said, with genuine surprise.

The obvious answer was no. This was Al Ankhara, not the United States. It was part of an alliance known as The Nations. All countries in The Nations were rich beyond measure; each sported skyscrapers in their cities, but also in each a traditional way of life existed side by side with the new.

"As you said, I met her last night. She is young and attractive."

"I would say she is beautiful, Khalil, not simply attractive."

"You've seen her, then?"

"Of course. I met with her and her party yesterday. Briefly, just long enough to be sure her father had not lied. There will be an exchange of money in this marriage but Butrus made it clear he would only accept a bride who met a standard of beauty. Fortunately, the woman does."

"Why is she traveling with such a small party? And why haven't you granted her the palace's full hospitality?"

"I deemed it safer that no one know of the marriage plans for as long as possible. You surely are aware there are those who would wish to prevent it from taking place."

He did, of course. Butrus's enemies. Omar's enemies. Even his father's enemies.

What of Layla? Would she wish to prevent it? Was that the reason she'd walked into the sea last night? Had she been trying to kill herself or, impossible as it seemed, swim to freedom?

"And the woman?" he said carefully. "You didn't answer my question. Does she know anything about her bridegroom?"

The sultan shrugged. "She knows he is rich. Beyond that, I have no idea. As we both know, it doesn't matter. Whom she marries is Omar's decision."

"Yes, but—"

"There is no 'but'," the sultan said sharply. "This is not the West, my son, it is Al Ankhara and she is of our people. She has been raised to respect her father's wishes." He paused. When he spoke again, his voice had taken on a thread of warning. "As have you."

"Why don't you tell me why you called me home, Father?"

"I have a task for you. A vital one."

Icy fingers seemed to brush down Khalil's spine. "And that task is?"

"You asked why the woman, Layla, travels with such a small party. I told you it was for her safety."

"You mean," Khalil said carefully, "it was for the safety of the planned alliance."

The sultan shrugged. "It is the same thing."

It was, by the standards of an earlier century but not, perhaps, by the standards of this one—or by the standards of a beautiful woman who was about to be given in marriage to a man who would surely make her skin crawl.

A man who would put his filthy hands on her soft breasts, whose diseased mouth would cover hers, whose grotesque body would possess hers night after night.

Khalil got to his feet. None of that mattered. The marriage, the marriage bed, had nothing to do with him. All the points his father had made were valid.

"And?" he prompted.

The sultan sighed and rose, too.

"And, I'm afraid the wedding is no longer a secret. Rumors of it are everywhere. Anything could happen, but nothing must. The woman must be delivered to Butrus as planned."

"You fear a raiding party. An abduction."

"Or worse."

More images raced through Khalil's head, scenes of brutality and carnage. Of Layla, pleading for her honor and for her life.

But she would not beg.

She would fight to her last breath, as she had fought him last night. Last night when she had twisted in his arms, when he had felt her body hot against his....

"These things must not happen. Surely, you see that, Khalil."

Khalil took a steadying breath. "Did you call me home to advise you? I'm sure your ministers have already done that."

"Have they?"

"Certainly. An alternate plan is simple to devise. All you need do is increase the size of the traveling party. Fifty men. One hundred. In dress uniform, of course, with lances, and riding the finest horses to honor tradition, but all of them armed with modern weapons to make it clear that they are unstoppable. What? Why are you shaking your head?"

"No horses," the sultan said impatiently. "No medieval nonsense. Why would we do that?"

Khalil barked a derisive laugh. "Because this *is* medieval nonsense," he said harshly. "We both know that."

"There is a much simpler and more effective way of guaranteeing royal protection to the woman, Khalil, one that no man will dare ignore."

"And that is?"

The sultan put his hand on Khalil's shoulder. "You are my son, heir to the Throne of the Lion and the Sword. You are the crown prince, the sheikh of Al Ankhara, protector of all its people."

The icy fingers swept over Khalil's spine again.

"Father—"

"You shall escort the woman to meet her groom."

Khalil jerked back. "No."

"Your plane will fly you and her to the city of Kasmir. As is traditional, Butrus will meet you there."

"Did you hear what I said? I will not—"

"You will have men with you, of course, just as you described them, in dress uniform but actually an assault team carrying modern weapons." The sultan smiled, obviously pleased with himself and his plan. "Not that you will need them. Butrus will be impressed. Your presence will make it clear that the match has the blessing of our house. No one will dare lift a hand against you and the throne you represent."

"This is out of the question," Khalil said sharply. "I have an important negotiation waiting for me in New York."

"There is nothing more important than respect for your country."

"Acting as an errand boy to deliver a woman who's been sold to a renegade has nothing to do with respect for my country!"

"You are being given a great honor. And no one has been sold to anyone."

Khalil snorted. "Tell that to yourself, Father, not to me."

The sultan's face darkened. "You forget yourself," he said, his voice colder than Khalil had ever heard it.

A muscle in Khalil's jaw flickered.

"Father," he said in as reasonable a tone as he could manage, "I'm sure your ministers think this is a good plan but—"

"The plan is mine."

"All right," Khalil said, even though he didn't believe it, "it's yours. But—"

"But," his father said brusquely, "it goes against all your Western sensibilities."

"No. Yes. Damn it, there are other ways. Not just to get her there. To secure an alliance."

The sultan folded his arms. "Name one."

Name one. Name one. Khalil ran his hands through his hair, until it stood up in small, black-as-midnight tufts.

"Offer Butrus money. Omar, too. Pay them to declare peace."

"Money is not the same as a blood tie."

"Gold, then. Diamonds. Oil. We have incredible riches—"

"Are you paying any attention at all? Treasure is nothing when measured against the bonds formed by blood. This marriage will take place, and you will be the bride's escort."

Silence filled the space between the men. Khalil understood the importance of filial duty, of princely obligation, but he had left home at eighteen, spent four years taking his undergraduate degree at Harvard, another taking a graduate degree in business at Wharton.

There had been some discussion about all of that. Jal, one of his father's senior ministers, had disapproved.

"There is always the danger, sir," he had warned, "that the prince may begin to favor the ways of the West over the ways of Al Ankhara."

The sultan had declared that nonsense. So had Khalil.

Now, and not for the first time, he could feel himself torn between the old ways and the new. More than that, he was to be an integral part of something he knew was wrong. To force a woman into a marriage she surely could not want...

"The woman knows what is expected of her."

Khalil looked up. Had he spoken aloud or were his thoughts so clearly written on his face?

"She has agreed to it?"

"She has." The sultan's expression turned wry. "Do you think this is a hardship for her, Khalil? I assure you, it is not. She is pleased, though she is clever enough not to show it. Consider what awaits her. The status of being Butrus's wife. His wealth. His power. Those things will become hers."

Only if Butrus permitted it, Khalil thought. The woman, Layla, would really be little more than his slave.

"Talk to her yourself, if it will make you feel better."

"No," Khalil said sharply. "I have no wish to—"

"My lord."

Khalil spun around. The two women he had seen on the beach and the thug who called himself a bodyguard had appeared on the crushed-marble path. They fell to the ground in respect—and revealed the woman who stood behind them.

Layla.

She had been beautiful in the moonlit night. Now, with the sun on her, Khalil could see that she wasn't beautiful.

She was exquisite.

Her hair was the color of wild honey, streaked with what looked to be a dozen lighter tones of gold. Her eyes were enormous blue pools tipped with thick, dark lashes. Her nose was small, her mouth full, the features delicately set in a slightly triangular face. It gave her the look of an elegant feline. Her body, not hidden by a man's *djellebah* but encased instead in a long gown of ivory silk, was lushly female.

Khalil's response was as swift as it had been the prior night. He felt himself harden, felt the sudden thrum of the blood in his veins.

"Show respect to the prince and the sultan, girl!"

His glance flew past her. Omar al Assad, her father, stood behind her, his face drawn into a ferocious scowl. He slapped his hand on her shoulder; Khalil heard the hiss of her breath, saw her wince as she dropped to her knees.

A growl sounded in his throat. He started forward but the sultan put out a hand and stopped him.

"I have brought Omar to the palace so he may be informed of our new plan, Khalil. As for this—" the sultan shrugged "—a father disciplining his daughter," he said mildly. "It is nothing."

Omar nodded. "She is headstrong, but she will learn. Butrus will see to it. Isn't that right, girl?"

Layla lifted her head. Her eyes glittered. With what? Defiance? Anger? Mockery?

"Are you deaf? Answer me when I speak to you!"

"She heard you," Khalil said coldly. "We all heard you."

"Your Highness." Omar's voice, directed at Khalil, was silky smooth. "We are honored to know that you will escort my daughter to her wedding."

"I have not said that I would."

"But your father assured me—"

Khalil walked slowly to Layla. "Look at me," he said softly. He put his hand under her chin and gently raised her face until their eyes met. "Do you know what is about to happen to you?"

"Answer the prince," Omar snarled.

Khalil silenced him with a look. Then he gazed into Layla's eyes again.

"Do you know?"

She nodded.

"Have you agreed that it should happen?"

"She does not need to—"

"My father, the sultan, tells me that you have agreed. Is that so?"

Did her mouth tremble? Omar stepped forward. She flinched, and Khalil gave the man a look that made him turn pale.

"I am speaking to your daughter."

"I only wish to remind her to show respect to you, my lord."

"Move away, Omar al Assad. I do not want you standing next to me." The man's mouth thinned but he did as commanded. Khalil knelt before Layla. He heard the gasps of those around him but he ignored them. "Answer me," he said quietly. "Have you agreed to this wedding?"

There was a long, long silence. He watched the tip of her tongue sweep across her lips. It was a very pink tongue, a delicate one, and he almost groaned at the unconscious sexuality of the simple gesture.

"Speak freely, Layla. You are safe here."

Again, the tip of her tongue swept across her lips. *"Na'am,"* she said quietly.

Yes, she'd said…and there it was again, the accent he'd noticed last night. For some reason it troubled him. So did her answer. It more than troubled him. It disappointed him, but why?

She had been raised in the old ways. She believed in them. And, as his father had pointed out, there was the promise of riches, of status.

Khalil rose to his feet.

The sultan was right. He had no role in any of this except as crown prince. He had obligations to meet and, in meeting them, he could at least ensure that this woman reached Kasmir safely. His father wished it. The council wished it. Omar wished it.

And so did she.

He turned his back on her, spoke directly to the little group gathered around them.

"I will escort her to Kasmir."

His father beamed his approval. So did her father. The two men began talking, but Khalil couldn't take his eyes from Layla.

Her posture was one of supplication but when she looked up, her eyes told a different story. As before, they glittered. With defiance, with anger…

With an unspoken plea?

He hesitated. Then he held out his hand. She took it, started to her feet—and stumbled. He caught her by the shoulders to steady her but she fell against him anyway. He felt the quick brush of her body and then she was on her toes and her lips were at his ear.

"For God's sake," she hissed, "are you blind? They're

lying. Your father. My father. Damn it, can't you tell that I've been forced into this?"

Khalil blinked. She was steady on her feet now, standing with her head bowed, making no protest as Omar stepped forward, cupped her elbow and marched her away. It was almost as if nothing had happened.

But something definitely had.

Her whispered words had not been spoken in Arabic.

They had been spoken in flawless American English.

CHAPTER THREE

LAYLA'S keepers—it was the only way to describe them—led her away. The thug first, then Layla with one woman on either side, then Omar, bringing up the rear.

Khalil stood staring after the little procession.

Had he really heard what he thought he'd heard?

No. It was impossible. The woman could not have spoken in English. Perfect American English. No accent, no stress on any but the correct syllables. And *what* she'd said, what he *thought* she'd said, was even more impossible.

"Khalil?"

Lies? Lies, told him by his father? That Omar would lie was no surprise. The man had a reputation for craftiness and there were times the word was nothing but a synonym for dishonesty.

But his own father… Would he lie?

"Khalil? I'm talking to you!"

The bitter possibility of duplicity crept into his bones.

His father might lie. He might do whatever he thought necessary for the good of Al Ankhara. Or the lies—if they were lies—might have begun with his ministers. Khalil suspected that Jal and his allies would not be above twisting facts when it served their purpose.

He'd tried telling that to his father more than a year ago but the sultan had refused to hear it.

His ministers' sole concern was protection of the throne, he always said. Khalil saw their actions as an attempt to maintain the status quo. It was why he had rejected much of the so-called advice they'd given him over the years.

He'd chosen Harvard over the smaller universities they had recommended, studied finance rather than foreign affairs, opted to remain in the States to run his family's investment conglomerate instead of returning home and taking the position of liaison the ministers had wanted to create for him.

"Liaison," he was certain, would have meant becoming their puppet. He'd long ago made up his mind not to be used by them.

Was he being used now?

"Khalil!" His father clasped his shoulder. "Pay attention when I speak to you."

Khalil took a breath and did his best to put a noncommittal look on his face.

"Sorry, Father. I was, ah, I was—"

"You were thinking about the woman." His father smiled. "I understand. She is beautiful. You would not be a man if you did not notice."

"She is beautiful, yes, but—" *But why does she speak like an American? Why does she say you lied to me?*

The words were on the tip of his tongue. Somehow he managed to keep them there and to match the sultan's knowing smile with one of his own.

"But she is not quite what she seems, Khalil. Perhaps you should be aware of that."

Khalil's pulse quickened. Here it was. The explanation he needed.

"Isn't she?" he said, as casually as he could.

His father shook his head. "She is woman with, ah, with wayward tendencies."

What did that mean? Was she not a virgin? That was important here.

"Wayward?"

His father nodded. "She has been a problem for Omar. She flaunts rules. She speaks of independence."

"And yet, she has agreed to marry Butrus."

Just for a second the sultan looked uncertain.

"Well, yes. Omar says she has repented."

"And Butrus knows she has been difficult in the past?"

"No, certainly not. It is one of the reasons Omar is so pleased. He secures an ally, does a service for the throne and finds a husband for a daughter who is a problem."

"By burdening his old enemy with a woman no one else would want," Khalil said coldly.

"Butrus wanted a woman who is beautiful. He is getting one."

"And what of the woman? What happens to her when Butrus realizes he's been duped?"

"Jal and I discussed it."

"Jal," Khalil said, even more coldly.

His father leaned close. "Omar says her mother was a sorceress. Perhaps she is, too."

A sorceress, Khalil thought with contempt. Among some of his people, that was an ancient and easy way to label a woman as evil.

"That's nonsense," he said brusquely.

His father shrugged. "Either way, Omar and Jal agree that she can take care of herself."

"No matter what Jal claims," Khalil said, "he is not the sultan."

His father's face darkened. "Nor are you. Not yet. And I do not have to explain my actions."

It was true. Besides, what good could come of this discussion? Plans and promises had already been made

"My apologies," Khalil said smoothly. "I only meant that you are Al Ankhara's ruler, not the council."

"A wise thing to keep in mind." The older man's expression softened. He chuckled and dug an elbow lightly into Khalil's side. "Imagine that sly fox, Omar, with such an attractive daughter! Who would have thought it? I asked him where he'd been hiding her and he said he had done precisely that. Hidden her to keep her from her willful ways, until the time came when he could give her to the right man as a wife." The sultan clapped Khalil on the back. "Thank you for agreeing to help us. Some of my ministers feared you'd become too Westernized to undertake this mission."

"Jal, you mean."

"I know you don't like him, but Jal wants to do only what is best for our people."

"As do I," Khalil said quietly, "whatever it may be—and however unpopular it might make me."

His father nodded. "Good. I will send our plan to you. Read it, then meet with us in the council chamber in an hour.

Khalil returned to his rooms. A servant brought him a leather portfolio.

It contained the council's plan for Layla's delivery to Butrus in Kasmir. Khalil leafed through it and almost laughed. The plan was twenty pages long, each page stamped with the embossed seal of the sultan, but it could have been condensed to one cogent paragraph.

Khalil's plane would make the trip carrying him, Layla and the original wedding party, augmented by three dozen of the sultan's personal guard. The plane would land at Kasmir where it would be met by Butrus and his men.

A couple of hours ago, he'd have simply refused to take part. But things had changed.

Last night Layla had walked into the sea in a desperate attempt to get away. He was convinced of it. Today, she'd said he was being fed lies, and she'd said it in English.

Now he had learned she was not truly a desirable bride.

The bottom line was that Omar saw her as a throwaway gift. If Butrus felt the same way, the so-called peace arrangement would lie in ruins. The sultan would lose face. And Layla would die. Butrus would kill her and no one would raise a hand to stop him. Such things still took place in some parts of Al Ankhara.

Was his father blind to all those possibilities, or didn't he care?

Khalil tossed aside the council's plan, shot to his feet and paced his sitting room. He could not let any of it happen. Damn it, he *would* not let it happen!

Twenty minutes and a few cell phone calls later, he had his own plan ready—but he would only implement it after assuring himself that Layla wasn't trying to play him for a fool.

And there was only one way to make that determination.

Layla was being kept in the harem.

That was a surprise. The harem had not been used in decades. His father had not changed many things after coming to power but he had changed the practice of taking concubines. One woman, he had said, was headache enough for any man.

Khalil had often wondered if that was because his father had loved his mother or because he hadn't. He supposed he would never know the answer; his mother had died when he was an infant.

The harem was connected to the main portion of the palace through a heavy wooden door. He couldn't recall it ever being locked, but today it was. He had to pound on it several times until someone—the thug—opened it.

The man was obviously not happy to see him.

"No one is permitted here."

Khalil eyed him coldly. If ever there had been a time for the nonsense of antiquated titles, this was it.

"I am not 'no one,' I am Sheikh Khalil, Crown Prince of Al Ankhara. Stand aside."

He brushed past the man without waiting for an answer and headed briskly down the corridor. The thug fell in behind him.

A second surprise.

He'd often played here on rainy days when he was growing up. He remembered rich tapestries, polished marble floors, gilded furnishings and frescoed walls. All those things were still in place but they had not stood up well to the ravages of time. The harem was dark and dreary; it smelled of mildew and age.

He thought of Layla, spending her days and nights here, and felt his jaw tighten as he swung toward her guard.

"Where is your mistress?"

"She is safe."

"I didn't ask you that. Where is she? I wish to see her."

"You cannot see her. It is forbidden. She is betrothed. She belongs to—"

"Do you want to die the death of a thousand cuts? Where is she?"

Hate burned in the man's tiny eyes but he jerked his head toward a closed door.

Kahlil strode toward it. Part of him was on the alert; part wanted to burst out laughing. The death of a thousand cuts? What bad movie had that come from?

Any desire to laugh vanished the moment he opened the door and saw Layla.

She stood within the confines of a room that had once surely been elegant. Now the couch behind her was covered with a grimy blanket; the walls were gray with age.

And yet Layla, standing straight and tall, hands fisted at her sides as if she were ready to take on the world, was magnificent.

She made his breath catch.

Her hair spilled like liquid sunshine over her shoulders. The day, and the room, were warm; her skin held a glint of moisture and the ivory silk gown clung to her body like a lover's gentle kiss.

"What do you want?"

She said it in Arabic. Now, though, he could definitely tell that it wasn't her native tongue. And though her voice trembled, she delivered the question with a rebellious lift of her chin.

"The council sent me to tell you its plan."

"Do I look like I give a damn about its plan?"

"Nevertheless, you will listen."

"To hell with you and the council! I will not—"

"You will do as you're told," Khalil roared.

"My lord," Ahmet said, "I'll deal with this."

"I will deal with it," Khalil snarled. "Alone."

He slammed the door in the thug's face. Then he moved quickly toward Layla, shook his head and put a finger to his lips.

"Now," he growled, raising his voice enough so the man outside the door would hear him, "you will behave yourself, woman."

Deliberately, she turned her back to him. Khalil clasped her shoulders and spun her around.

"Did you hear what I said? Behave yourself, or—"

She flew at him, all fists and nails. He grabbed her hands, folded them against his chest.

"Stop it!"

"Bastard," she hissed, "*mad al haram!* You no-good, despicable—"

Her words were all-American, and his reaction was all male. There was only one way to silence her and he took it, lifting her to him and capturing her lips with his.

She struggled. She fought. He kept kissing her, told himself it was the best way to keep her quiet.

Told himself that, even as he felt himself drowning in her taste, her scent, her heat.

"Don't fight me," he whispered, against her lips.

And, for one amazing moment, she obeyed. Her body softened. He let go of her fists and gathered her in his arms, bringing her tightly against him. Her lips softened, too, and parted just enough so he could slip the tip of his tongue into her mouth and savor its sweetness.

Savor it, until he felt the sharp bite of her teeth.

Khalil cursed, jerked back and dragged his handkerchief from his pocket. He put it against his lip, looked at the tiny crimson smear on the creamy white linen—and laughed.

Layla stared at her attacker in disbelief. She'd bitten him and he'd laughed? Maybe she was losing her mind. It was the only thing that made sense.

What had happened during the past week must have done it.

She had been lured to Al Ankhara. Taken prisoner. Threatened. Tormented. Told, explicitly, what awaited her and told, too, that she would accept it or pay the price for disobedience.

Now a stranger who thought he owned the universe had kissed her and she…and she had—

Her breath caught.

She had let him kiss her. Let herself lean into his strength, let herself feel the power of his embrace, the thrust of his erection against her belly…

The doorknob rattled.

"Lord Khalil?"

The man—the prince, Lord Khalil—slapped one hand against the door and pulled her to him with the other.

"Who are you?" he said in a low voice.

Layla gasped with surprise. He was speaking English. He'd understood her, then. When she'd spoken to him in the garden this morning, the desperate words had tumbled from her lips in English. She hadn't realized it until a long time after, and then her heart had shriveled at the realization that she'd wasted her one possible chance to get help, even worse, that she'd broken the vow she'd been forced to make not to reveal the truth about herself.

"I asked you a question. Who are you?"

What to tell him? What to say? What risks were worth taking? The door shuddered again; her eyes went from it to his face. He looked cold and dangerous. And he'd kissed her as if he owned her.

But Butrus *would* own her, unless a miracle happened.

"Answer," he growled, "or I'll step away from the door and let the pig outside handle things."

She licked her lips. Khalil felt his gut tighten. Even now—furious at himself for the moment of weakness when he'd kissed her, the door shuddering under the strength of a knife-wielding brute—even now, damn it, he couldn't keep from watching that simple motion as if his life depended on it.

"Last chance, sweetheart," he said, and that easy use of the American word did it. After all, Layla thought, what more did she have to lose?

"My name is Layla Addison. Omar was my father."

"Lord Khalil!" The door shuddered again. "Open this door or I will call for the guard!"

"*Was* your father?"

"*Is* my father, but he didn't raise me. My mother is American. Twenty-three years ago she was here, in Al Ankhara, and he…he stole her. She escaped. I was born in the States, raised there…please, please, I beg you, get me out of this terrible place!"

It was an unbelievable story, but then, everything that was happening was unbelievable. Back in New York, Khalil could have verified it within a day. He'd have contacted his attorney, hired a private investigator, gone to see Layla's supposed American mother.

Here all he could do was believe her, or see her as a liar.

Another bang against the door. Another shouted warning from the man on the other side of it.

"If this is true," Khalil hissed, "what are you doing in Al Ankhara?"

"It's a long story," she said, with a wild-eyed glance at the door.

And no time to tell it, Khalil thought grimly.

"Lord Khalil! If you do not open this door…"

Khalil stepped back. The door swung open; the thug all but fell into the room. His beady eyes went from Khalil to Layla, then back again to Khalil.

"What is happening here?"

"Do you dare question me?" Khalil said coldly.

The man hesitated. "I only meant—"

"I am taking the woman to the council. You will remain here."

Khalil grasped Layla's arm and hurried her away. She stumbled as she tried to keep pace.

"Where are we going?"

"To meet with my father's ministers."

"What for?"

"To save my father from making a terrible mistake."

"I don't give a damn about your father! What about me?"

"You are the mistake. Can't you move any faster?"

"What are you going to do?"

"I'm going to get you your freedom."

"How?"

"Just do as you're told."

"But—"

"Is it beyond you to obey a simple command? Be quiet. Say nothing. Do nothing. I have a plan."

Well, he did—except, it hadn't involved kissing the woman. No matter. The incident changed nothing. The kiss had been a matter of expediency, that was all. And yes, perhaps she had responded. So what?

She was beautiful. He didn't believe in sorcery but he did believe in a woman's ability to use her feminine wiles. And he was a man, with a man's hunger. Add a touch of mystery, of danger, and it took little to start a fire.

But the conflagration had been momentary.

Sex was exciting, a function of the body and the senses, but the emotions sex roused were controllable. A man was a man. A woman was a woman. Biology, even passion… but not uncontrollable emotion.

He had kissed the woman, but it wouldn't happen again. That wasn't the problem. Getting her out of here was the problem.

But he had a plan for that, and it was a plan that would work.

At least, he hoped it would.

He paused in the great entry hall of the palace only long enough to place one final, confirming cell phone call.

Then he hurried Layla to the council chamber. The ministers and his father were waiting for him. They rose when he entered, looking as shocked to see Layla walking demurely behind him as if he'd entered the room accompanied by a lioness.

"What is the meaning of this?" Jal said sharply.

Khalil ignored him. He had already told Layla what to expect, how to behave, to seem obedient and respond to nothing anyone said, including him.

Could she manage that?

He turned to her now, his eyes filled with warning. "Stand away from me," he said coldly.

Her eyes flashed, but it was so quick he was sure nobody else had noticed.

"Yes, my lord," she whispered in Arabic, and she swallowed hard, stepped back, cast her gaze downward and folded her hands.

Khalil almost grinned. It was an excellent start.

"Khalil," Jal said again, "I asked you a question. What is that woman doing here?"

Khalil looked at him. He had never believed in titles, in the nonsense of showing respect to one. Jal, however, did. All these men did…even, perhaps, his father.

Now he would put that to his advantage.

"I am the crown prince," he said in a voice that rang with command. "You would do well to remember that and to address me properly."

Silence filled the room. Jal glanced at the others, looking for support, Khalil knew, and found none.

"My apologies, sir. It is just that the presence of the woman has taken me, has taken us all, by surprise."

Khalil held his gaze for a long moment, then turned to the sultan. He walked to the long table at which the council sat, to where his father sat at the head of it, and placed the leather binder containing the council's plan before him.

He had always known he would someday assume leadership of Al Ankhara, even though it was not something he wished for, and that he would institute changes when he did. Until then, he'd told himself, he would not act in opposition to his father.

That had all changed.

The truth was, he'd spent a third of his life pretending he wasn't really of this place. But it was time to admit that he was, and to keep his father from a being part of a disastrous plan that could only bring grief to the throne and the nation.

He took a deep breath. One final try.

"Father," he said quietly, "I have read the plan."

"And?"

"And it is not a good one."

He heard the buzz of the ministers' voices. His father held up his hand.

"Why not?"

"The immediate outcome might seem beneficial but once the plan is fully implemented…"

Jal got to his feet. "We thank you for your opinion," he said in a voice as smooth as butter, "but we've already determined what to do if you did not wish to act on our behalf."

"And that is?"

"We will go forward without you, my lord." Jal smiled. "It is not a problem."

Khalil nodded. So much for one final try.

"You didn't let me finish," he said pleasantly. "I *do* wish to act on your behalf. On my country's behalf, I should say. And I've thought of a way to do just that."

He could see relief in his father's face, suspicion in Jal's.

"Go on," his father said.

"It is not appropriate to take a willing bride to her groom in such a manner."

"Is that what the woman thinks? If so, perhaps Your Highness should remember that her opinion has no meaning."

Khalil heard a strangled sound from behind him. He looked over his shoulder. Layla had raised her head; her eyes were dark with belligerence. He shot her a warning look, waited until she dropped her gaze, then turned toward Jal again.

"Of course it hasn't," he said calmly. "But transporting her in a troop carrier might make a poor impression."

"A troop…" Jal smirked. "One would hardly call your plane a troop carrier, my lord. Besides, these are not troops, they are an honor guard."

"Semantics," Khalil said dismissively. "The point is, we want a show of strength but we also want to show that the full support of the kingdom is behind this wedding. Is that not why you've asked me to escort the bride?"

Silence, even from Jal. Khalil knew he had him in a corner.

"What is your suggested change?" the sultan said.

"A woman, veiled and cloaked, and a man of my height and coloring will fly with the soldiers."

"And you and the woman?"

Here we go, Khalil thought.

"I have arranged for a second aircraft to carry us. Only us. We will leave here an hour after the plane bearing the honor guard is en route, and no one but those in this room will know of it."

"For what reason?"

"For a variety of reasons, Father. The most obvious is that if anyone intends to make an attempt on the woman when the plane lands, their efforts will be wasted. Also, this way we will ensure that the men waiting on the ground for her are loyal to the throne. Last, we will avoid Butrus possibly taking offense at seeing his bride escorted by a coterie of armed men."

The sultan looked thoughtful. Jal, however, looked furious.

"You made arrangements for this aircraft, for this plan, without consulting the council?"

"I saw no reason to consult you," Khalil said with cool conviction. "Must I remind you again that I am the crown prince? Consulting you is a courtesy. The only approval I need is my father's."

Jal's face turned red. The others looked from him to the sultan. There was a silence, and then the sultan cleared his throat.

"It seems to me Khalil's idea makes sense."

Khalil nodded. "I'm glad you see it that way."

Very glad, he thought, as the meeting came to an end, because the next time these men saw him, they might very well call his plan an act of treason.

CHAPTER FOUR

THE ministers filed from the council chamber.

Each man paused before Khalil and bowed. It was a traditional sign of respect.

In the past, Khalil had usually waved such gestures away. Now he stood quietly and accepted acknowledgment of his authority. From this moment on, it would be vital that they saw him as the heir to the throne, as a man due the kind of homage he'd always thought out of place in today's world.

But this was not today's world. It was the world of Al Ankhara, and here, like it or not, custom meant power and power meant that maybe, just maybe, he could pull off what came next.

His father was the last to leave.

"My son," he said softly. The sultan glanced at Layla, standing like a statue against the wall. "We have given you an enormous responsibility. One you would have preferred to avoid."

The men's eyes met.

"Yes," Khalil said. "But I see that I must do it."

For the first time in years, his father embraced Khalil and kissed him on both cheeks.

"Have a safe journey."

"Thank you, Father."

The sultan touched Khalil's arm and left the room. Khalil waited until the corridor was empty. Then he turned to Layla.

"I assume you heard everything."

Her head came up. "I heard you talk about me as if I were a thing, not a woman."

Despite himself, Khalil felt a smile ease across his face.

"I assure you, no one in this room forgot that you are a woman."

"A sexual object, you mean. Or maybe a sexual commodity."

"And you think you are more than that?"

He knew it was a low blow the second the words left his mouth. She didn't deserve that; whether she'd deliberately responded to his kiss or not, he had instigated it. It was just that the situation infuriated him. That he should have been drawn into such a squalid mess.

"You know," she said in a low voice, "you look American. You sound American. But you're the same kind of…of barbarian as the rest of these people."

"These 'people'," he said carefully, "are *my* people. Watch what you say about them."

"It's the truth. You're no better than they are. Buying and selling women—"

"No one has bought you yet," Khalil said harshly. "But if you keep angering me, that might just happen."

Her mouth trembled. For all her display of temper, she was terrified and he, damn it, wasn't making things any easier for her.

He thought of drawing her into his arms, stroking her golden hair back from her flushed face and telling her everything would be all right, but he wasn't fool enough to do it. For one thing, the assurance could well be wishful thinking. For another, it would surely be a sign of weakness. A sign that Jal might be right.

Perhaps he had become too Westernized.

His plan could only succeed if he established firm control. Of the woman. Of the situation. The sooner she accepted that, the better.

"If you want to get through this," he said, "stop debating and start moving."

When she didn't stir, he made an impatient sound, put his hand in the small of her back and propelled her toward the door. She wrapped her hand around the back of a chair and dug in her heels.

"Get through this, how?"

"I'll explain when we're alone."

"Alone? You and me?"

"Alone," he said firmly, "you and I."

She gave a brittle laugh. "Now you're going to correct my grammar?"

"Listen to me, woman—"

"I have a name."

"What you have," he told her grimly, "is a bad sense of timing. You want to discuss my plan? Fine. But not here and not now."

Layla narrowed her eyes. "Do you know what 'out of the frying pan and into the fire' means?"

Khalil let out an exasperated breath.

"It means, keep on with this nonsense and I might just change my mind about helping you."

"Helping me? You just told your buddies that you're going to deliver me to Butrus!"

"Woman. There will be time to talk later. Now is a time for action."

"I told you, I have a name! And if you really think I'm going to put myself in your hands without any idea of what you're going to do to me—"

A shriek burst from her throat as Khalil jerked her off her feet, slung her over his shoulder and marched out of the room.

"Put me down! Put…me…down!"

She punctuated each word with a blow of her fist against his back. Khalil shifted her weight and kept moving.

"Keep that up and you'll regret it."

The warning only made her hit him harder but he ignored the blows and made his way up the stairs, hoping they would not encounter anyone. Luck was with him; they passed only a servant who blinked at the sight of her prince transporting a woman like a sack of laundry but showed no other reaction.

He was the crown prince, after all.

And if he wanted a woman badly enough to carry her away, who was a servant to argue?

Khalil slammed the door to his sitting room behind him, strode into the bedroom and dumped his still-shrieking burden on the bed.

The instant she hit the mattress, she rolled away. He grabbed her, tossed her into the center of the bed again. When the same thing happened two more times, he cursed, captured her wrists, flung her back against the pillows and came down on top of her, pinning her to the bed with the weight of his body.

"Stop it!"

"Is that what this was all about? Getting me into your bed?"

"You flatter yourself."

"Because if it is—"

"It isn't. Trust me, *habiba*. If I wanted you, I would simply take you."

He spoke with such cold assurance that Layla believed him. Out of the frying pan, indeed, she thought, and struggled even harder.

"Keep moving like that," he said tightly, "and I might just change my mind."

God, he was right! In her desperate attempts to fight him off, she'd managed to mimic all the motions of sex, her hips lifting to his, her back arching as she rose to him.

And he…he had responded. She could hear the rasp of his breath, see the darkening of his eyes…feel the surge of his erection against her.

Layla went still. "Get off me," she said in a thready whisper.

"It will be my pleasure."

"Get off!"

He sat back. "Behave, or I'll tie you to the bed. Do you understand?"

He waited until she gave a grudging nod. Then he stood up and she scrambled back against the pillows, her eyes following him as he paced the room.

"I didn't mean—" she hesitated "—I didn't mean for that to happen."

He swung toward her, an insolent smile on his lips.

"For what to happen, *habiba?*"

"You know damned well what I mean. I was— I was only trying to stop you from—"

"From what?" His mouth thinned. "From trying to save your neck?"

"Are you? Because that isn't what you told those ratty old men."

He tried not to smile at that. It was a perfect description of the council.

"I told them what they wanted to hear."

Layla swallowed dryly. "But did you mean it?"

Khalil lifted one dark eyebrow. "Perhaps you've forgotten the council's charge."

"But I thought—" she hesitated "—I thought you said…"

She couldn't bring herself to go on. Had this all been a game to torment her? Anything was possible in this horrid place.

"If you're not going to help me," she said, trying to keep her voice from quavering, "tell me now instead of letting me hope."

"If I said I would help you, it was a misstatement."

Layla felt her heart plummet.

"Keeping my father from taking a disastrous action is what matters." He looked at her, his face cruel and cold. "You're simply the beneficiary of that."

She sat straight up, her eyes locked to his. "Are you incapable of saying what you mean? Are you delivering me to Butrus or aren't you?

"I am not. Doing so would be a huge error. My father doesn't see that right now, but I do. And, when this is over, so will he."

Layla shuddered. "Thank you. For a minute, there, I thought—"

"Don't," he said sharply. "Don't thank me. And don't think. That is not your function. Just listen, do as you're told and we might both get what we want from this. Can you manage that?"

"Why do you speak my language?" Her voice broke. She was filled with a combination of fury and despair so potent it was hard to draw breath. "Because you're not anything like me or anyone I know."

"You're right. I'm not anything like you or anyone you know, *habiba*. Keep that in mind. I will not take you to Butrus, but that doesn't mean I have to get you out of Al Ankhara, either. Is that clear?"

It was. Terrifyingly clear.

"Answer me, woman. I hold your life in my hands. Tell me you will obey me without question or this ends, here and now."

Layla lifted her head and looked at him through a blur of tears.

"I understand. Completely."

Did she? Khalil doubted it. If she really had grown up in the States, she could no more understand her situation than a kitten could understand what would happen if it were put in a cage with a python.

He needed her to be obedient, yes, but he also needed her to behave herself.

That thing that had just happened in the bed.

It could be…distracting.

He wasn't interested in bedding her, despite the way she'd moved against him. The way she'd fought, then melted when he'd kissed her. Even the way she'd stood facing him in the moonlight, her wet *djellebah* clinging to her body, outlining every curve…

But yes, it was distracting, and he couldn't afford distractions now.

The last thing he needed was to look at her and wonder what she looked like under that length of ivory silk. He'd waste precious time if he imagined the taste of her. Of her breasts, her throat, her nipples.

Would they be sweet on his tongue? Would she cry out in abandon when he sucked on them?

Would the skin of her thighs be like satin? Would the entrance to her womb grow hot and wet when he cupped her?

God, he was losing his mind!

Biology. Just basic animal instinct. That's all it was. End of story. End of attraction. All that mattered was getting both of them out of this mess with their heads still attached to their necks, and it had to be done quickly.

Luck had been with him during the meeting with the sultan and the council. He had presented his plan—what they now believed to be his plan—and it had been accepted, but for how long? Jal was clever; given enough time to think about it, he might well decide the course Khalil had charted was not to his nefarious advantage.

Khalil looked at the woman in his bed. She sat watching him with almost preternatural caution, as if she couldn't decide whether to call him Satan or saint.

'Sheikh' would do, he thought grimly. It would establish, and quickly, his right to control her every action.

He tore his eyes away, went to his dressing room, grabbed a handful of garments, tossed some to her and dumped the rest on a chair.

"Get dressed."

She looked at him in bewilderment. "I *am* dressed."

"Use the dressing room, if you wish."

"I said, I *am* dressed."

His gaze swept over the ivory silk gown. Layla struggled to keep from wrapping her arms around herself. How could a glance from those pale, cold eyes make her feel so naked?

"You can't travel in that."

"Travel where? You said you weren't taking me to—"

"Get dressed," he snapped, "or I'll do it for you."

Eyes flashing, she reached for the clothes he'd thrown at her and sorted through them. Men's things, all of them. A white tee. A blue chambray shirt. Faded jeans.

"You want me to wear these things? They won't fit."

"I'm sure the fashion police will forgive you," he said with an unpleasant smile.

"And there's no underwear here. I can't—"

"You can. And you will."

She glowered at him. He glowered back. She tossed her head and rose from the bed.

"I'll need a belt to hold up the jeans. And what about shoes?"

What, indeed? He looked at her feet, bare and delicate in thinly heeled gold sandals. His own shoes would never do; they'd fall off her the second she tried to walk.

"Find a belt in the dressing room. Forget about shoes."

"I can't walk without—"

She gasped as Khalil reached for her arm and pulled her against him.

"Such a short memory, *habiba*. No thinking. No questioning. Just do as you're told. Remember?"

"Or what, Prince Khalil? You'll have me beaten?" She lifted her chin in what he was coming to recognize as an all-too-familiar gesture of defiance. "I've already survived that."

His eyes narrowed. "Are you claiming someone beat you? Who was it?"

"Never mind. It doesn't matter now. Besides, you've admitted you need me as much as I need you. You can't save your father from making a mistake if you lock me away in a dungeon, now, can you?"

"There are other ways to control a wayward woman," he said, part of him cringing at how he must sound, part of him angry enough not to give a damn. He swept his hand into her hair, cupped her head and tilted it back, forcing her posture to betray her vulnerability even if she refused to do it with words. "Shall I list them for you, *habiba?*"

She didn't answer. He brought his face down to hers.

"You have no cards to play. The sooner you accept that, the better your chances of survival."

"Once," she said through her teeth, "a very long time ago, after my mother told me my father was from your country—though not how he'd come to be my father—I decided I should learn a little of my so-called heritage."

"Don't tell me," Khalil said sarcastically. "You bought a romance novel about sheikhs and maidens and believed the nonsense that filled its pages."

"It took years, but one day I decided to study your language," Layla said, ignoring the remark. "Unfortunately, I didn't learn much."

He raised an eyebrow. That explained her shaky command of words but not their full meanings.

"Maybe I didn't study long enough. Or hard enough. Or maybe, instinctively, I knew what had happened to my mother in Al Ankhara and my mind blocked out the language spoken in this backwater hellhole."

Khalil wound her hair around his hand.

"Be careful, *habiba.* I don't take insults lightly."

"But I did pick up some choice phrases, not from my teacher but from a guy in the class. He knew words the instructor didn't."

"So you've already proven."

"Not entirely. I've just remembered some others." She smiled sweetly. "For instance…"

She spat a phrase at him. And waited.

Khalil worked the words over in his mind. It took a

few seconds because, at first, they didn't make sense. Then they did.

If he was right, it made the things she'd called him before seem tame.

But she'd gotten the verb wrong. The noun, too. Instead of telling him to do something physically impossible to himself, she'd pretty much told him to make intimate friends with a goat.

Despite everything—the mess they were in, the danger to his father and the throne—it made him want to laugh.

Except he knew what a mistake that would be.

Her tone, the fire in her eyes, the very fact she'd thought to say such a thing to him, were all direct challenges to his masculinity and his authority.

He knew, too, that there was only one way to react that would have any meaning for her.

"Don't be silly, *habiba*," he said softly. "Why would I do that by myself when I could, instead, do it with you?"

Then he bent to her and captured her lips with his.

She tried to hit him but he'd expected that and he tugged on her hair, still wound like a golden cable around his fist, drawing her so close that her upraised hands were trapped between them.

She whimpered, tried to knee him, but he was too close. He shifted his weight, used his strength and sent them both staggering back against the wall and when he was pressed hard against her, he let go of her hair, framed her face with one hand, cupped her bottom with the other and hoisted her off her feet.

She gasped. Good, he thought in taut fury…

And then, without warning, his body responded.

His blood pounded in his veins. His penis filled, hardened, pulsed with desire…

He moved against her. Moved again.

She cried out against his plundering mouth and he held her closer, took the kiss deeper—and suddenly she moaned and became soft as silk in his arms.

It was what he had been waiting for. Her wordless admission that he was master here. If they were to survive, she had to be subdued, to admit that he was in charge.

It was a timeless way of taming a woman, one he'd never ascribed to even if, at this moment, he understood its value.

But her moan, her pliability, changed all that.

He forgot the reason he'd kissed her, forgot everything but the taste, the heat, the feel of Layla in his arms.

"No," she whispered, "no, don't…"

Even as she said those words, she was moving her hands up his chest, over his shoulders, winding her arms around his neck. She rose to him, rose against him, let the silken tip of her tongue dance against his.

Khalil groaned.

He lifted her higher; she twisted one leg around his. He dragged up the hem of her gown, felt her skin cool against his questing palm, and the sexy little cries she gave as he stroked his hand up her calf, to her thigh, started a roaring in his head.

He kissed her throat. Bent his head and kissed her breasts. Sucked the aroused, beaded nipples into his mouth through the ivory silk. Let the urgency of her soft cries make the blaze inside him burn even hotter.

"Layla," he whispered, and she thrust her hands into his hair, kissed him back, kissed him with as much passion as he felt.

He swept her into his arms, his mouth hot and hungry on hers, carried her quickly to the bed…

Tap, tap, tap.

A sound. A noise. Someone knocking at the sitting room door. He heard it the way a man hears something in a dream. But it wasn't a dream, because it persisted, and a voice was added to it.

"Sir?"

It was Hassan.

Layla went still in his embrace, but only for a heartbeat. A second later, she began flailing her arms, knotted her hands into fists, fought him like a wildcat while her eyes blazed with rage.

"Get away from me," she hissed, "damn you, get—"

He slapped his hand over her mouth. "Quiet!"

"Mmmph," she said, "mmph…"

His other hand curled around her throat. "One more sound," he warned, "and it will be the last sound you make!"

He heard the hiss of her breath, felt her lips clamp together. He waited. Then he lowered her to her feet and opened the door.

Hassan almost fell into the room.

"Sir! A plane has landed. Not here, but at the airport. The pilot sent a message. He says—"

"He says he is waiting for me."

"Yes, my lord. But I do not understand. What of your own plane?"

"Listen to me, Hassan. Do you know the old entrance to the courtyard? The one I used as a boy?"

His old servant nodded.

"If there is a guard there, get one of the women to lure him from it."

"How, sir?"

"Use your imagination, man! Tell her to offer him food. Drink. Something. Can you manage that?"

"If you wish it, sir, but I don't understand. Your plane—the one that always brings you here—is to take off any moment. You are on it, sir. You and the lady, but—but you are not. You are here. I knew you must be because—"

"Hassan." Khalil grasped the old man's bony shoulders. "You will pretend I am on that plane. The lady, too. Once it is gone, the lady and I will leave by the old courtyard entrance. You will have a car waiting for us. No one must know any of this, Hassan. No one. Do you understand?"

The old man's eyes were filled with questions, but he was too well-trained to ask them. Instead he grasped Khalil's hand and brought the back of it to his forehead.

"I will do as you ask, sir."

"Thank you," Khalil said softly.

Hassan made one of those impossible bows and backed away. Khalil shut the door and brushed past Layla, who stood watching him with cold eyes.

"Touch me again," she said, "and, so help me, I'll kill you!"

He looked at her. Her face was pale, her lips pink from his kisses. The damp imprint of his mouth branded the silk over her still-budded nipples.

He wanted to tell her she had nothing to worry about, that he would never touch her again, that he had only done it to make a point…

He wanted to sweep her in his arms, take her down into the softness of his bed, tear away the silk that covered her and finish what they had only just begun.

Instead he turned his back and reached for the pile of clothes he'd left on the chair.

"Get your things off," he said brusquely, "and put on the stuff I gave you."

"Damn it, I'm talking to you! I said, touch me again and—"

"You'll kill me." He swung toward her, his expression impassive. "I heard. And I'm terrified. Now, get moving."

"I am not one of your women, Prince or Lord or Sheikh or whatever it is you think you are."

"I do not think I am any of those things. I *am* those things. And no, you are not one of my women or you would know better than to argue with me. For the last time, get dressed."

"I am not a dog, either, or a horse, or a creature you can order around, and...and...what are you doing?"

"I'm changing my clothes," he said calmly, as he unbuttoned his shirt and tossed it aside. His hands went to his belt. "You want to stand there and watch, that's fine." His belt buckle opened; so did the zipper of his fly. "I'll undress you myself after I'm—"

Layla grabbed the stack of clothes from the bed and flew into the dressing room. Khalil laughed.

And then he stopped laughing and wondered what in the name of Ishtar he'd gotten himself into.

CHAPTER FIVE

WHAT had she gotten herself into?

Layla slammed the dressing room door and tossed the stuff Khalil had given her on a chair.

Forget joking about going from the frying pan into the fire because it wasn't a joke. It was the absolute, incontrovertible truth.

This morning she'd been a woman on the verge of being owned by an ogre. Now she was a woman owned by a tyrant.

No, she thought, and blew an angry breath, no, that was wrong. He didn't own her. Nobody did. Nobody ever would.

Yeah. Right. He didn't own her, but he might as well because if she didn't follow his orders, she'd never get out of this horrid place. She knew it. The trouble was, so did he.

"Damn it," Layla said, and shoved her hands into her hair, jamming the wild strands back from her face as she began pacing the length of the dressing room. A good thing it was the size of her entire apartment back in New York. Almost that size, anyway. Because, like any caged animal, she needed to walk off her frustration.

Frustration? Rage was more like it.

If only she'd never come to Al Ankhara. If only she hadn't gotten tangled up in all that stupid "know thyself" crap. If only she hadn't somehow convinced herself that the way to bury twenty-three years of anger at the man who'd fathered her, the man who'd played no part in her life and only a vicious part in her mother's, was to confront him. To see for herself the truth of what her mother had told her, that her father, his people, his very nation were evil and barbaric and...

And, he'd done his best to prove it.

Pretending he was glad to see her. Inviting her to stay in his home so they could get to know each other. Saying he regretted the past and maybe, just maybe, his side of the story wasn't as bad as her mother had made it sound.

No. It was worse.

She'd awakened one morning and he was more than the beast her mother had so brutally described. She was, he'd told her, going to make up for the humiliation her mother had caused him more than twenty-three years ago.

"You are my daughter," Omar had said coldly. "An asset which I have been denied. Now you will make up for it. Butrus will pay me for you, and the sultan will thank me for securing peace."

She didn't know what that last part meant, but the first part meant he'd sold her, and he told her about the man who'd bought her in excruciating detail.

He'd described Butrus's brutish looks, his cruelty, his outlaw status. When she'd begged him not to do this to her, he laughed.

"Are you not your mother's daughter? She incurred this debt. You shall pay it."

Layla had tried to come up with something to change his

mind. She would report him to the authorities. That had
made him laugh even harder. She'd buy her freedom. Another joke. In the midst of it all, he'd asked if she was a virgin.

What was the best answer? "Yes," she'd said, and saw
the first glimmer of hope.

Surely, not even he would give his daughter's innocence to a monster.

"Excellent. Butrus will pay twice what I asked him."

That night, she'd slipped out of Omar's compound and
run into the desert. His men found her a day later, ex-
hausted and dehydrated. He had her whipped. When she
recovered, she told him she'd lied about being a virgin.

His face had darkened with anger.

"I told Butrus that you were. He agreed to pay a
virgin's price."

"There's more," she'd said, and wove a tale about her simple, go-to-school, go-to-work existence that made it sound
like she led the wayward life of a sulky tabloid heroine.

At first she'd thought he would kill her. Then his expression had turned wily.

"It doesn't matter. By the time your bridegroom learns
the truth, it will be too late."

"But you said—you said marrying me to him would
secure peace."

"Peace," he'd said, and laughed. "What it will secure is
a small fortune for me."

Things had moved swiftly after that. The pig with the
knife and the two women who had taken pleasure in her
anguish set off with her on a journey that was to end with
her marriage.

And then, last night—was it only last night?

Layla scooped up the things she'd dropped on the chair
and sat down.

Last night she'd made one last attempt at freedom or, who knew, maybe an attempt at ending the nightmare the only way she could. A man had stopped her.

A man so beautiful, so masculine, she'd thought about him throughout the long hours that had followed. And when she'd been brought to him this morning, when she'd blurted out what was happening to her in a language he shouldn't have known and, incredibly, he'd understood...

She thought he would be her savior.

A sob of anger, of frustration, of despair rose in her throat.

Stupid. Stupid, stupid, stupid.

Her savior had turned out to be just a different kind of jailer, never mind that he spoke English and had pale-gray eyes. He was a sheikh. A prince. Beneath a sleek coating of Western sophistication he was as arrogant and cold as everyone else in the place.

And her blood bubbled with heat whenever he kissed her.

"Layla!"

She jumped as his fist pounded against the dressing room door.

"Two minutes, or I'll come in and dress you myself."

He would, too. He was vile enough to do it. As for kissing her...

"Damn it, woman, do you hear me?"

Layla shot to her feet. "A dead man would hear you!"

"Two minutes. You understand?"

She understood, all right. She absolutely understood. And if he tried to kiss her again, she'd do what she'd told him she'd do.

She'd damn well kill him.

"Is this your idea of a disguise? Because if it is, I don't think much of it."

Khalil looked up as Layla emerged from the dressing

room. His eyes swept over her, from head to toe. She was right. His clothing was much too large for her; he'd expected that. But he'd hoped it would help her look like a boy.

It didn't.

What she looked like, in his shirt and jeans, was every man's dream of hot, wild sex.

Her hair was a tumble of sun-shot gold. His blue chambray shirt hung open, revealing the white cotton tee beneath it, and the tee revealed…

"Don't look at me that way!"

"If you flaunt yourself," he said coldly, "I will look."

"I'm not…"

He looked at her again. At her breasts. She could feel her nipples tighten, and she said something under her breath, grabbed the edges of the shirt and dragged them together.

"Now there's nothing to look at," she said with a toss of her head, "unless you're a complete idiot."

She was right. There *was* nothing to look at. He knew it, logically, but what did logic have to do with seeing her like this? The shirt. The jeans. His jeans, hanging precariously from her hips, the faded denim drooping against the carpet. Flaunting herself?

The truth was, she should have looked foolish in this get-up.

Instead the clothes were a reminder of the woman hidden under them. Of the breasts that he had cupped with his hands. The long legs that had felt like silk under the stroke of his palm. The knowledge that what touched her skin now belonged to him.

How could something so simple carry a sexual intimacy so powerful?

To hell with the plane waiting on the airstrip. With the

risks they were about to take. To hell, too, with his rapidly growing doubts about her, the questions he should have asked but hadn't.

Like, how had she come to be in Al Ankhara in the first place? The sultan had hinted that she knew all about Butrus, that he was the worst kind of brute, but she'd been willing to tolerate him because he was rich.

Was it true? Had she thought it over and changed her mind after the marriage had already been arranged?

Anything was possible. He knew it, and didn't give a damn.

He wanted to sweep Layla into his arms. Carry her to his bed. Strip her naked so that she was exposed to his eyes, his hands. His mouth.

He wanted to touch her everywhere. Kiss her everywhere. Taste her breasts again because that first time could never be enough. He wanted to savor the texture of her skin, relish the sweetness of her nipples on his tongue, watch the shock of desire in her eyes when he slid his hands beneath her, lifted her to him, exposed her hidden flesh so he could kiss it, lick it, suck it into the heat of his mouth.

A shudder racked his body. He turned his back and drew a long, steadying breath. If this continued, he was going to explode. And that was insane. His hunger for her meant nothing. Saving her was simply the only way to save his father from continuing in a direction that would bring disaster.

He swung toward her again. "You're correct, *habiba*," he said briskly.

Her eyebrows rose.

"You will not fool anyone in that outfit. Even a eunuch would know you are a woman."

Layla nodded and slapped her hands on her hips. The

chambray shirt fell back. Khalil felt his body tighten. If she knew how she looked, why didn't she do something about it?

"Button the damned shirt," he said, more sharply than he'd intended.

"What?"

He strode toward her, reached for the shirt and roughly yanked the edges together.

"Close it. Show some decency."

Her mouth dropped open. "Decency? Decency? You come from this place and you talk about decency? Are you crazy?"

Probably, but if he was, she was the cause.

"If you don't want people to see that you're female," he said grimly as he began closing the buttons, "do something to hide the evidence."

Layla flushed a dark pink. "I don't need your help."

Khalil ignored her. His knuckles brushed lightly over her breasts. Not deliberately, he assured himself, damn it, not deliberately, but the clenching in his belly told him he was a liar—and the budding of her nipples told him he wasn't the only one having a reaction.

She pushed his hands away. "Don't."

Her voice was unsteady. Why did that give him so much pleasure?

"Don't what?" he said with a calm he didn't feel. "Remind us both that you are not the innocent Butrus was led to expect?"

Her hand flew through the air; he grabbed her wrist before her hand reached its target, and dragged her to her toes.

"Be careful, *habiba*. It is not wise to lose your temper

with the only man who can save you from your prospective groom's tender ministrations."

"You're saving your father and your precious throne, not me," she said, panting a little as she strained to break free of his grasp.

"Whatever, it will be to your benefit." He narrowed his eyes. "Unless you're having second thoughts about walking away from Butrus's money."

"You," she said, through her teeth, "you, almighty sheikh, are a miserable son of a bitch!"

"Am I?" His mouth twisted; he lowered his head until they were eye to eye. "How did you end up in this situation, *habiba?* Would you like me to think your father flew to America, kidnapped you and brought you to Al Ankhara?"

"Do you? Really think?" Her lips curved in a mirthless smile. "I'm surprised your brain is capable of such a feat."

His eyes narrowed. "Push me," he said softly, "and you'll pay."

"I'm paying already by being here."

"That's not an answer to my question. How did you get yourself into this mess?"

"Would you believe me if I told you?" She laughed at the look on his face. "No," she said, "you wouldn't."

She was right. The answer didn't matter anyway.

He was, just as she'd said, not doing this for her. He was sure the council's plan would not solve problems on the northern border but might only make them worse, and if the world learned an American woman had been forced into marriage with Butrus, Al Ankhara would suffer. There'd be diplomatic repercussions. Investors would shy away. And the budding tourist industry would collapse before it even got started.

What tourist would set foot in a place where women

were virtually sold into slavery? It was morally wrong. Al Ankhara had moved past the old ways. He could not, would not, let it tumble back through the centuries.

"We're wasting precious time," he said sharply. "We're stuck with each other. If you want to escape this in one piece, you'll do well to obey me without hesitation."

"Giving orders. That's what you're good at. You and your people."

"Me and my people?"

His voice carried a warning but Layla was too angry to give a damn.

"Exactly. You're all the same. You snap out commands. You subjugate women. You strut around as if you own the universe. Well, it won't work with me. I don't obey, I don't bow my head in submission, I don't—"

"You don't know when to shut up," Khalil growled, and gathered her to him and kissed her.

Layla gave a little grunt of protest but his arms bound her to him and when she tried to twist her face away, he thrust one hand into her hair and kept her where he wanted her.

It was a kiss of pure male domination, given without mercy, a reminder of his power and her servitude…

Until he tasted the salt of her tears.

The realization that she was weeping went through him like a knife. Twenty-four hours at home and he was changing into a man he didn't know, forcing himself on a woman who was frightened, kissing her because it was an age-old method of subduing a rebellious woman.

Kissing her because the taste of her was as sweetly drugging as wine.

"Don't cry," Khalil said softly. "*Habiba*. Don't weep, sweetheart. I won't let anything happen to you."

She gave a sad little hiccup and he framed her face with his hands, lifted it to his and kissed her again, his mouth moving gently against hers, sinking into the velvet warmth of hers, silk against silk...

And what in the name of Ishtar was he doing? There was no time for this nonsense, and nonsense was all it was, the befuddled thinking of a man too long without a woman's body moving beneath his.

Khalil thrust her from him. She swayed, blinked, and for a moment what he saw in her eyes made him want to gather her to him again. But her eyes cleared, turned hard and brilliant as sapphires, and she slammed the back of her hand over her lips and wiped away his kiss.

"You're a barbarian," she said, "just like everyone else in this godforsaken country!"

He narrowed his eyes. "Perhaps you should keep that in mind, *habiba,* since it's this 'barbarian' who holds your life in his hands."

He could almost see her searching for a clever response, but how could she find one that wouldn't be a lie? He *did* hold her life in his hands. His, too, though she didn't know that yet.

"What?" she said. "What are you thinking?"

"I'm thinking that hair of yours is a dead giveaway." He stalked into the dressing room, came out holding a dark blue cap. "Tuck your hair up under that," he said, tossing it to her.

"Did you ever hear of the word *please,*" she said, so sweetly it made his teeth ache.

"Did you ever hear of following orders?"

Her chin rose. She swept her hair up with one hand, jammed the cap on her head and tossed off a brisk salute.

He wanted to laugh but he knew that would be a mistake. He hadn't taken her for the pleasure of her company. Still, he couldn't deny she was not just beautiful but tough and courageous—and the sooner he got her out of his life, the better.

"Let's go," he said, and put his hand in the small of her back and shoved her toward the door.

Khalil was not a pessimist, but he was a realist.

Why fool yourself into pretending things would go well when you had every reason to believe they wouldn't?

He had made plans as best he could. He'd arranged for his private plane to take off first, with a man and woman disguised as Layla and him onboard. He'd made sure that the second plane was ready and waiting at the airport, not at the palace's private airstrip. He'd disguised Layla and himself as Western tourists.

Still, he put a warning finger across her lips as they stepped into the hall. The look she gave him suggested she was tempted to sink her teeth into it. Despite himself, he grinned. Then he took her hand, ignored her attempts to tug it free and hurried her downstairs and out the unguarded door.

The car he'd asked for was waiting with Hassan himself at the wheel. Khalil tried not to wonder when the old man had last driven a car—or, in fact, if he could.

"Good," he said, as he settled into the backseat beside Layla. "Stop at the gate."

"The guards?"

"The ones on duty are loyal to me and will ask no questions. After that, do not stop again until we reach the old turnoff for the airport."

Hassan nodded. The car lurched forward. When they reached the gate, the old man slowed to a stop, the guards peered inside, saluted Khalil and motioned the car on.

"Quickly now," Khalil said.

Hassan stomped hard on the gas pedal, and the car shot forward like a rocket, leaving a trail of dust behind it. Twenty minutes later they were on the old turnoff, which bypassed Al Ankhara's new, modern terminal.

The chartered plane waited on the tarmac, the pilot lounging in the open door, a half-smoked cigarette between his fingers.

Khalil got out, offered his hand to Layla. She hesitated, then put her hand in his and they ran to the plane and up the steps to the door.

The pilot dropped the cigarette and straightened up.

"Sheikh Khalil?"

Khalil nodded. "How fast can you get this thing off the ground?"

A quick grin, a quicker salute, and the pilot disappeared into the cockpit.

Moments later they were airborne.

CHAPTER SIX

THEY took off so quickly that all Layla had time to do was stumble into a leather love seat.

"Buckle your seat belt," Khalil said brusquely, and when she didn't comply fast enough to satisfy him, he reached over and did it for her.

"I'm perfectly capable—"

"Perhaps we'll have the opportunity to discuss those capabilities in detail at some point, *habiba*. Right now my sole concern is keeping you in one piece."

She knew that. He had to protect her so he could protect his father. That was the reason he was doing this.

Why should that bother her so much?

Layla took off her cap—*his* cap—tossed it aside and turned her face to the window.

She was expendable, a means to an end, and that was fine because he was the same thing to her. Those quick moments of heat in his arms were all but predictable when you considered the circumstances. She was riding an emotional roller coaster. That made anything possible. She'd been a psych major before she'd switched to archaeology; she knew all about things like Stockholm syndrome, where a captive fell for her captor.

Especially a captor like this one.

Tall, wide-shouldered, with those incongruously pale eyes, those high cheekbones, that blade of a nose and a body that could be a promo for a Manhattan gym. Add in the way he spoke English, as if he'd been born to it but with a gorgeous accent that was probably the gift of a private tutor, and what you had was one very, very sexy man.

But nothing could disguise what he was.

A predator, wild and dangerous, never mind the educated speech and the Armani or whatever-it-was suit she'd first seen him wearing, or the jeans and T-shirt he wore with careless grace now.

She'd boarded a plane with an egotistical stranger who was part of a culture in which women were second-class citizens, and she had no idea what would happen next. Khalil hadn't given her the chance. Besides, she'd been so relieved to know he'd help her that nothing else had mattered.

A cold knot formed in her belly.

All at once what came next mattered. A lot.

What was his plan? Where was he taking her? Not to the States. She didn't know much about planes but it didn't take an expert to figure out that this one wasn't capable of making the endless flight home. The jet was luxurious, all pale-gray carpet, black leather seats and bright-red cushions, but it couldn't possibly hold sufficient fuel for a twelve- or thirteen-hour journey.

Then, where were they going?

She had to ask, even though she didn't want to. Asking questions about her future was an absolute admission that he was in charge of her life, but then, she hadn't been in charge of it since coming to Al Ankhara.

A hand fell lightly on her shoulder. Layla started, looked up and saw Khalil standing in the aisle beside her.

"You can relax now. We're safe."

She watched as he shrugged off his denim shirt. Her eyes followed the motion. The roll of his broad shoulders. The flex of his biceps. The taut lines of his washboard abs under the clinging cotton tee as he tossed the shirt on a seat.

Her throat constricted. Safe? She wouldn't be safe until she was in New York and he was thousands of miles away.

"What does that mean? Don't you think they'll send someone after us?"

He sat down beside her and stretched out his long legs.

"Yes, but not for a while. My own plane—the decoy plane—will land and there will be some confusion." An understatement, but why go into that now? "When the second plane carrying us does not arrive, my father and the council will spend some time trying to figure out what happened. They'll have to locate the company from which I rented this plane, get the details of our flight…"

"Delaying tactics," Layla said.

Khalil nodded. "Exactly. By the time all that happens, I'll have contacted my father and explained things to him."

"Explained what? You can't think he won't care when you tell him you aren't turning me over to Butrus!" She hesitated. "Because you aren't. Right?"

He looked at her, a hint of sardonic amusement in his eyes.

"Do you think this is all some elaborate scheme to deliver you to your bridegroom anyway, *habiba?* Don't worry. It isn't."

Layla moistened her lips. "It's not that I didn't believe you…"

"Of course it is."

He grinned. It was such a disarming grin. Charming. Almost boyish. Add that to the sexy good looks and…

And, what did that have to do with anything? Layla cleared her throat.

"It's just that you haven't told me anything."

He nodded. "I know." He rose, went to the rear of the plane and reappeared carrying a wicker basket which he set on a small table. "We can talk while we eat."

"I'm not hungry."

"Of course you are." He sat down again, opened the basket and took a thermos, porcelain mugs, plates, linen napkins and foil-wrapped packets from its interior. "You haven't eaten in hours."

"It's kind of you to think of it, but really—"

"Kindness has nothing to do with this. The flight is a long one and I have enough to deal with without considering that you might be about to take a Victorian swoon."

So much for charming. "I'm not given to swoons, Victorian or otherwise. And you owe me answers."

He looked at her through narrowed eyes. "You have that wrong. I owe you nothing." He pushed a small plate toward her, then placed one of the foil packets on top of it. "I'll answer your questions because it's necessary. First, though, eat that sandwich."

For one wonderful moment, she imagined bashing him over the head with the plate, but what for? It wouldn't change the facts. He held all the cards in this game. Maybe it was better to try and keep on his good side.

Layla unwrapped what appeared to be a turkey sandwich, neatly cut in quarters. She looked up. Khalil was watching her, arms folded over his chest. She rolled her eyes, picked up a piece of the sandwich and bit into it.

The first taste, and her stomach growled in eager response. He was right; she hadn't eaten in hours and her belly knew it. She looked at Khalil. If he so much as smiled, she really would bean him. But he only nodded in approval, unwrapped a sandwich of his own and began eating.

She ate everything he put in front of her. The sandwich, then a small container of yogurt and, finally, a small cluster of grapes. He poured them both cups of steaming tea; she drank down half of hers, then blotted her lips with a napkin—and found him watching her.

"What?"

"Nothing. There's just… You have a bit of yogurt on your lip." He leaned toward her. "Just…there."

His warm, slightly rough and altogether masculine finger touched her mouth. Her heart seemed to leap into her throat.

His eyes turned the color of midnight except for a thin, pale blue ring around the pupils. What would he do if she touched the tip of her tongue to his finger? If she drew his finger between her lips, sucked it into the heat of her mouth?

Layla jerked back.

Constant stress. Little sleep. Not much food. Add all that together, anything was possible. All the more reason she needed to keep her wits about her.

"I am perfectly capable of taking care of myself," she said, snatching her napkin from her lap and wiping her lips with it.

"If you were," he said, his tone as cool as hers, "we wouldn't be in this situation."

"What's that supposed to mean?"

"It means that I still don't know how you got yourself into this."

"Why not ask Omar and your father?"

An excellent question, and he would ask it of his father as soon as they were safe. They weren't safe yet, despite what he'd told Layla. They wouldn't be safe until he spoke with his father and convinced him that what was happening was as it had to be.

Inshallah, he thought. It was a concept steeped in tradition, and he could only hope it was one of the traditions to which his father adhered.

"Cat got your tongue, Your Highness?"

Khalil put everything but their cups of tea into the basket and set it aside.

"How this happened is no longer meaningful," he said. "How we deal with it is."

"And just how are we dealing with it? Where is this plane taking us? When will I go home?"

"It's taking us to Paris."

"Paris?"

"That's what I said."

"You mean, to an airport in Paris, where I can get on a flight to New York and—"

"No."

"What do you mean, no? I told you, I want to go—"

"I have an apartment in Paris."

"So what? I don't want to go to your apartment. I want to go home."

She knew she was behaving like a petulant child. But that smug arrogance of his, that look on his face that said he knew everything, that he was king of the universe, was infuriating.

"Believe me, *habiba,*" he said coldly, "I want the same. The sooner you are out of my life, the better."

"Then why—"

"Because I say so," he snapped, "that is why."

Layla's lip curled. She swept her arm across the table and sent both cups of tea flying. The liquid splashed over Khalil's shirt and jeans.

For a few seconds no one moved. The air in the cabin seemed to grow electric.

"*Laa tatalaa'ab ma'ii,*" he growled, grabbing her by the shoulders. "I warned you, woman. Do not mess with me!"

Apologize, her frantic brain said. Just say you're sorry. Except, she wasn't. He deserved what had just happened and more.

"Nothing to say, *habiba?*" His eyes hardened. "If you behave like a five-year-old, you should be treated like one. I'm half tempted to put you over my knee."

Heat flooded through her. She knew what he'd said had no sexual meaning. Still, it conjured an image that swept everything else aside.

She could see herself lying not over his knee but in his arms, both of them naked, his hands on her bare skin, his fingers hot, his mouth even hotter.

Color swept into her face.

She jerked out of his grasp, bent and scooped up the porcelain cups. Her hair swung forward against her cheeks. Good, she thought desperately. Maybe it would hide the blush she knew reddened her skin.

"Leave it!"

Khalil had risen to his feet. Now, he bent down, curled his hand around her wrist and tugged her up beside him.

"Did you imagine I could just carry you away from your father and your bridegroom? That I could go against the direct wishes of the sultan and his ministers without any repercussions?"

He felt the swift kick of her pulse under his fingers. He'd frightened her. Good. Did she think not marrying the man she'd been pledged to was like making a date and then walking away from it?

"What repercussions?"

"Your marriage was meant to solidify peace on the northern border. Your father and your bridegroom were to become allies."

"Don't call him my father," she said bitterly. "Siring a child isn't the same as raising one. And don't call that… that creature my bridegroom. It makes a mockery of the word."

There it was again, all that fire and outrage and courage. But where had those qualities been when the arrangements for the wedding were being made? Had she been forced into this, as she claimed, or had his father told him the truth?

Had she known what was going to happen, had she agreed to it and then changed her mind?

He told himself it didn't matter. He wasn't doing this for Layla. He didn't care if she'd been ready to give herself to Butrus for money and power or not.

He had to keep that in mind.

Khalil dropped his hand from her wrist. "I'm not interested in a philosophical discussion," he said coldly. "The only thing that matters to me is finding a way out of this mess so that everyone can hold up his head."

"His," she said bitterly. "The sultan. Omar. Butrus."

"I told you, *habiba*, we are not about to have a philosophical discussion. I must prevent bloodshed, and I need a couple of days to do it."

"How? I have the right to know, Khalil."

It was the first time she'd used his name. Ka-leel. He liked the sound of it on her lips. He'd heard many American women try and give his name what he supposed they assumed was an exotic sound but Layla was the only one who'd managed it…

And who gave a damn how she said his name? Khalil frowned and folded his arms.

"I will tell you what you must know when you need to know it," he said, and all but groaned at how idiotic he sounded. Why did this woman bring out the worst in him?

"Do you have any idea what *you* need to know?" She was all but breathing fire and, by Ishtar, her fury made her even more beautiful. "No? Then I'll tell you." She tossed back her hair, slapped her hands on her hips and narrowed her eyes. "You sound like an ass!"

"An ass, hmm?" he said, very softly.

She nodded. "And that's too bad, because, generally, I have nothing against—"

Khalil kissed her.

It was either that or do what he'd threatened a little while ago, put her over his knee, and not only was she not a child, he wasn't into that kind of thing.

But he was into women. Beautiful, fiery women.

Beautiful women were easy to find but none ever had the guts to stand up to him. Nobody did. People bowed and scraped and yes sir'd him half to death.

Not Layla, he thought, and then he stopped thinking, groaned, gathered her tightly against him and kissed her and kissed her until she gave a whisper of surrender, rose on her toes and wrapped her slender arms around his neck.

The kiss went on and on. Khalil slipped his hand down the waistband of her jeans, groaned again as he cupped her naked bottom.

"Oh, yes," she whispered against his mouth, "oh, yes…"

He slid his hand between her thighs. She was hot and wet and when she felt his fingers on her, she moaned and moved against them.

He threaded his free hand into her hair. Angled his mouth over hers. Nipped at her lower lip and soothed the tiny hurt with a stroke of his tongue. She whimpered, curled her fingers into his shirt, moved closer, closer, closer…

Hell, had he lost his mind?

Yes, he thought, answering his own question, he had.

Khalil lifted his head, let go of her and stepped back. She swayed, then opened her eyes. He watched them clear…

Watched them focus on him.

Watched the passion in them change to shock and then to something else. Disgust? Fear? Regret that the kiss had ended? He didn't know and he wasn't going to waste time trying to figure it out. There was more at stake here than a tumble into bed.

"There are blankets and pillows in that compartment," he said, as if nothing had happened. "I suggest you get some sleep."

He could see her struggling to regain her composure. Once she had, she stood straight and tall, brought her hand to her forehead and snapped off another salute.

"You're learning," he said with a tight smile. "But you might want to add a Prussian click of the heels to that salute."

"When hell freezes over."

Khalil thought about telling her to stop being so damned clever. Mostly, he thought about taking her in his arms again and finishing what they'd begun—but if a man didn't learn from his mistakes, he really was an ass.

And yet, even as he thought that, he wrapped his hand around the nape of Layla's neck and drew her to him for a quick, searing kiss. Then he walked to a seat far from hers, sat down and began working out precisely what he'd say when he phoned home.

One false move and instead of saving his father, he damned well might destroy him.

He had told Layla the flight would be a long one.

Long? It was endless. He'd flown the same route many times before but never with a kingdom on the line as well as a woman's life.

His, too.

But that went with being the crown prince. He'd always been fascinated by people's reactions to his title. Men were awed or respectful. Women saw it as sexy. He'd known one woman, a high-powered model, who'd insisted on calling him "sheikh" when they were in bed.

Even thinking about it made him grimace.

That relationship hadn't lasted very long.

He was a man. Just a man. He had obligations, yes, but he didn't want to be judged by the size of them. It was a simple desire, but by now he suspected it was an impossible one to fulfill.

People never treated him as if he were Khalil al Kadar. They treated him as the heir to the throne of Al Ankhara. No one ever permitted him to forget who he was, that he would someday assume a title that had come down through the centuries.

There were times he'd imagined turning his back on the burdens of his birth, but duty and honor were part of him. He'd always known, in his heart, that he could never walk away from his destiny.

Some of what he did was simple. He attended ceremonies, represented his country at diplomatic functions, made himself available for brief interviews when necessary.

He'd done more difficult things, too, taking over his family's investments, turning tens of billions of dollars into hundreds of billions of dollars and seeing to it that big chunks of the money went toward building a modern Al Ankhara.

Not modern enough, he thought, his mouth thinning, or this mess—an unwilling woman sold into marriage— wouldn't have happened, but he'd seen to it that children were being educated, that hospitals and clinics were built, that the wonders of the Internet were reaching even the smallest villages.

But there were things he'd sidestepped.

"Meet with my ministers," his father had said, "not whenever you can but on a regular basis, Khalil."

He hadn't. He was too busy. He was involved with other projects. He had a thousand good reasons to turn away from his father's request, partly because the thought of his father growing too old to rule was painful but also because he was not in any hurry to live the life of a sultan.

The rules. The restrictions. The traditions, many of which he knew were wrong.

He had discussed the problem many times with his two oldest friends. Tariq and Salim understood. Like him, they were sheikhs within The Nations; like him, they'd been educated in America. And they were, like him, often caught in the deep abyss between the old and the new.

But neither of them had faced a problem quite like this. A father who'd approved a series of damning events. A woman who had to be saved.

Khalil looked at Layla, in the love seat near the front of the plane.

A woman who might or might not have agreed to be sold into marriage. Who was not the docile creature her groom anticipated. Who was, nonetheless, the kind of woman a man dreamed of possessing.

His expression softened.

She was asleep now, but a couple of hours ago he'd noticed her head bobbing. There were pillows and a light throw on a seat near hers but she'd ignored them. He'd watched for a while, decided she was too proud for her own good and he'd snatched up a pillow and a blanket and brought them to her.

She'd reacted as he should have known she would.

"I don't want them," she'd said coolly.

"But thank you, anyway," he'd said, just as coolly.

"But thank you, anyway," she'd parroted, with a brilliant smile.

"Didn't anyone ever teach you to be polite?"

"You mean, didn't anyone teach me to be obedient?" She'd flashed another smile. "If you want blind obedience, Your Highness, get a dog."

He'd turned on his heel and gotten the hell out of there before he'd done something stupid. Still, she'd ended up using the pillow and the blanket. The pillow was tucked against the window; the blanket was draped over her from neck to toe.

The way she treated him, you'd never know he'd saved her pretty neck.

Well, hell. Khalil shifted uneasily in his seat.

He hadn't saved anything. Not completely. Not yet. Besides, hadn't he made it clear that what he was doing was not for her?

Except it was.

The thought of her in Butrus's arms. In his bed. The thought of that soft body frozen with terror under the renegade's filthy hands...

"Sir?"

He looked up, forced himself to look attentively at the pilot.

"We'll be landing in a few minutes."

Khalil cleared his throat. "Thank you."

"Jack—my co-pilot—and I hope the flight was to your liking."

"Yes, yes, it was fine."

The man started to salute. Something in Khalil's face stopped him; he dropped his hand to his side, nodded and headed back to the cockpit.

Khalil got to his feet, slipped on his chambray shirt and looked over at Layla. She was still asleep. He headed up the aisle to her.

"Layla."

She didn't move. He squatted down beside her.

"Layla. Time to wake up."

Still nothing. Khalil reached out, stroked her hair back from her face.

"*Habiba.* We're in Paris."

A sigh, soft as silk, whispered from her slightly parted lips and feathered over his skin. He looked at her for a long moment. Then he scooped her gently into his arms.

Another sigh. Her head drooped against his shoulder, her arm rose and looped lightly around his neck. He could feel the beat of her heart against his.

Did the earth suddenly shift? No. Of course not. It was only the wheels of the plane locking into place as they approached the runway.

Surely it was only that.

Khalil bent his head, pressed a light kiss to Layla's spill of silken hair as they landed. He wrapped the blanket more closely around her as they taxied to the terminal, then carried her to the door and out into the soft Parisian night.

CHAPTER SEVEN

SUNLIGHT, warm and soothing. Silk sheets, soft and sensual. A bed big enough to get lost in and the rich aroma of fresh coffee…

A bed big enough to get lost in?

Layla shot up against a sea of pillows. At home she slept on a pull-out, two-cushion sofa. One wrong turn and you tumbled onto the floor.

This was hardly that sofa.

This was a bed that made the term 'king-size' a joke. Emperor-size, was more like it. The linens would cost more than she earned in a month; the pale-yellow duvet seemed to float over her skin…

Her skin, separated from the sheets and the duvet by an oversize white cotton man's dress shirt, the sleeves too long, the tail too long, a shirt that surely had to belong to Khalil.

Why couldn't she remember anything? The plane. The night sky. A pillow under her cheek, a soft cashmere throw over her body, a man's arms holding her close. Khalil's arms. Khalil's lips against her hair. His heat, surrounding her…

Tap, tap, tap.

Layla stared at the door, her heart banging into her throat, the duvet clutched to her chin.

"Yes?"

Her voice quavered and she bit her lip in an effort to force sanity into her head. When dealing with a lion, you were dinner if you behaved like a mouse.

But it wasn't Khalil who opened the door and peeked into the room, it was a plump woman with graying hair and a tray in her hands.

"Bonjour, mademoiselle," she trilled as she approached the bed. *"Je suis Marianne. Avez-vous bien dormi?"*

"Marianne." Layla took a breath. "Do you speak English? *Parlez-vous anglais?"*

"Non, mademoiselle, je regrette, je ne parle pas anglais."

Great. The woman had no English. Layla had no French. Not enough to be useful, anyway. High school French was only a memory.

Stay calm, she told herself. Stay focused. And try again.

"Can you at least— *Est-ce que vous*— *Est-ce que vous* tell me, uh, tell me *où je suis?"*

"It's *où suis-je,"* an amused male voice said, "but that's not bad, *habiba.* For an American."

Khalil stood in the doorway, barefoot, leaning against the jamb with his hands tucked lazily into the pockets of a pair of well-worn gray sweatpants. He wore a matching T-shirt with HARVARD stamped across the front in crimson letters. Droplets of water glittered in his dark hair— apparently, he'd just showered—but he hadn't shaved and there was soft-looking stubble on his jaws and chin.

Very sexy-looking stubble. And she was huddled across from him with her bed-head hair and sleep wrinkles on her face.

Life wasn't fair.

And who cared? What he looked like, what she looked like, didn't matter.

Other things were more important. Like, where were they? Whose bed was this? And—a rush of heat sizzled through her blood—and who had undressed her and put her into it?

"You have questions, *habiba*."

It was a statement. Well, she'd never thought the sheikh of the universe was stupid.

"Lots of them," she said, trying to sound cool and detached.

He nodded, said something to the maid in rapid French. So he spoke three languages. So what? And he was gorgeous. Again, so what? Did he think that gave him the right to take command of her life?

Probably.

That, plus the fact that he'd gotten her out of Al Ankhara and to…Paris? Was this Paris?

Foolish question. Of course it was. She knew it as soon as Marianne threw open the glass doors that led onto a wrought-iron terrace. Layla saw flowering plants, a round table and two chairs and, beyond, a glimpse of a dark, slow-moving river.

Every guidebook in the world was filled with photos like this, but none could impart the city's special, early-morning fragrance or explain the way the sun's soft rays crept into the room and filled it with warmth.

Marianne set the table with the things she'd brought on the tray. A coffee service. A covered basket. A tiny ceramic butter pot. Flatware, linen napkins, a bud vase that held one perfect yellow rose.

Paris, absolutely, Layla thought, and for some foolish

reason, her heart seemed to take a couple of giddy dance steps.

The housekeeper stepped back into the room, dipped her knee to Khalil and sent Layla a shy smile, as if the sight of a woman in this bed were an everyday occurrence. Which it no doubt was, Layla thought as Khalil shut the door, then fixed his pale-gray eyes on her.

"All right. Ask your questions."

Foolish or not, she had to be certain. "Are we in Paris?"

"Yes."

"Where in Paris?"

He lifted an eyebrow. "Do you know the city, *habiba?*"

She didn't, but why admit it? "Do *you?* Or can't you answer the question?"

He grinned. "The Fourth *Arrondissement.*"

"Oh."

His grin widened. "To be precise, we're in an apartment in a sixteenth-century building on the Ile de la Cité, over-looking the Seine. Do you need the name of the street, or have I told you enough?"

"You think this is amusing? Being dragged from place to place like a sack of laundry?"

His gaze flickered over her. "You don't look like a sack of laundry," he said softly. "But I'm sure you're aware of that."

Though she still clasped the duvet to her chin, she blushed, which only made her feel more snappish.

"What I'm aware of is that I don't have any recollection of getting off that plane. Did you arrange to have something put in my coffee?"

"Exhaustion was in your coffee, *habiba.* I tried to wake you when we landed but you were—what's the expression? Out like a light."

"Then how—"

"I carried you." His voice grew husky. "In my arms, from the plane to the car that came for us, and then to my apartment."

Layla swallowed dryly. "And…and who put me to bed?"

"I did." The rush of crimson that suffused her cheeks made him decide to go easy on her. He loved seeing that rise of color; there was something about rocking her cool demeanor that gave him pleasure, but she'd been through a lot and she deserved to be handled gently right now. "Relax, *habiba*. I brought you to this bed but Marianne did the rest. That's what this inquisition is all about, isn't it?"

She nodded, and the tip of her tongue swept across her bottom lip. His gut knotted. Bad enough he'd slept in the room across from this one, tossing and turning most of the night as he imagined her here, in his shirt, in his bed. Seeing her now, still in that bed, her hair in sexy disarray, her eyes glittering…

He drew himself up straight. What was the matter with him? It was time to put the next part of his plan into action.

"Get up," he said brusquely. "Shower, get dressed. I'll wait for you on the terrace."

"Get dressed in what?"

It was a good question. Khalil scratched his head. "You'll have to wear what you wore yesterday. Marianne's probably washed everything. I'll tell her to bring it all to you."

"But what about shoes?"

"I'll see if she has some to lend you."

"But—"

"No 'buts', *habiba*. We have important things to do. Get out of bed. *Sortez du lit.*"

Layla shook her head. "Not with you in the room."

Khalil gave her a long look. Yesterday he'd cupped her breast. Felt the kiss of her nipple against his palm. He'd slipped his hand between her thighs, felt her heat blazing against his fingers. Last night he'd carried her from the plane in his arms. Held her in his lap as his driver drove his Mercedes through the sleeping city.

But he had not yet touched her with the slow, lazy strokes of a lover, the excitement building, time slowly unraveling as they learned the secrets of each other's bodies...

And they wouldn't, he told himself sternly. That was not what this was about. That he'd done those things to her before didn't mean he would do them again. Becoming her lover would serve no purpose. It would only further complicate an already complex situation.

He had only one objective. To keep his father and his country from irreparable harm. Saving Layla was the way to accomplish that, nothing more.

And exactly how many times have you had to remind yourself of that? a sly voice said inside him.

Khalil frowned. "You have ten minutes to get ready," he said brusquely, "not a minute more."

"Why? What happens after breakfast?" Anger made her forget to clutch the duvet. It fell from her hands as she glared at him. "You have no right to keep me in the dark!"

He looked at her. The fire burning in her eyes. The defiant lift of her head. The gorgeous mane of hair, flowing over the shoulders of his white shirt in a wild tangle, as if a man's hands—his hands—had threaded into it as they made love.

The need to take her crackled through his veins like an electric current. She wanted to know what happened next?

What he knew they both wanted to happen next, because there was only one way this could end, he thought, and he went to the bed, cupped her shoulders, lifted her to him and claimed her mouth with a soft, teasing kiss.

He heard her breath catch. Felt her hesitation. Then her arms snaked around his neck, her lips parted and clung to his.

Khalil told himself to let her go.

He had a plan. A timetable. And this was not part of it.

But, God, the taste of her. The feel of her. The woman scent of her…

Tap, tap, tap. The sound of the door, opening. And then Marianne's lilting voice.

"Pardonnez-moi, monsieur, mademoiselle, mais j'ai le jeans et le… Oh!"

The door slammed. Khalil and Layla jerked apart. Her face was pale, her mouth sweetly swollen. His heart was galloping as if he'd run a marathon.

Silence stretched between them.

"I didn't," she said in bewilderment, "I really didn't mean to—"

"No," he said, "neither did I." He bent to her again and brushed his lips gently over hers. "Get dressed," he said in a husky whisper, and followed it with the most difficult thing he'd ever done. He scooped the jeans and shirts from where his housekeeper had dropped them, tossed them on a chair…

And walked out of the room.

Paris. The city of romance. Of light. The city that was the fashion capital of the world, and she was strolling it in rolled-up men's jeans, a T-shirt and a man's blue shirt jacket. Plus the finishing touch. Laced-up sensible black shoes, two sizes too large, borrowed from a blushing Marianne.

Actually, that wasn't the finishing touch.

That honor belonged to the man walking beside her. Khalil, wearing mocs, light-blue jeans, a navy T-shirt and a black leather jacket, looking so gorgeous that women couldn't help but smile at him.

Then they looked at her, their artfully-drawn lips parted and their blusher-highlighted chins all but dropped to their elegantly clad toes.

Layla snorted.

The minute they'd left the marble lobby of the apartment building, she'd wanted to run back inside and hide, or at least grab a paper bag and jam it over her head on the ostrich theory. If nobody could see your face, they couldn't see the rest of you.

Khalil wouldn't let her. She'd taken a step back and he'd slipped his arm around her and drawn her close against him.

"You look beautiful, *habiba.*"

The man caught on fast, but he wasn't a very good liar.

"I look like a kid dressed for a Halloween party."

A grin lifted the corners of his mouth. "A charming description."

"An accurate one," she'd muttered, "and do us both a favor, okay? Don't insult my intelligence by trying to tell me I look beautiful."

"For all you know, everyone will think you're dressed in a style that just walked off the runway at Milan."

That had made her smile. "Oh, if only."

She'd tried not to react to the stares. It didn't matter how she looked, she'd told herself, but she hadn't believed it for a second. They had just turned onto Avenue Montaigne when a statuesque brunette who looked as if she'd just stepped out of a *Vogue* cover glanced at her, then at Khalil, and bit back a smile.

"Okay," Layla said, shooting the brunette an icy glare, "that's it. You said we'd do some shopping. When?"

"Very soon, I promise."

She heaved a sigh of relief. "I'll have to borrow some money from you. I don't have anything. No cash. No credit cards."

"Don't worry about it. Why don't we have breakfast first, since we seem to have, uh, skipped having it in my apartment? Then we'll find you something to wear."

Two teenaged girls coming toward them, dressed as fashionably as the brunette, looked at her, at each other, and giggled.

"We'll shop first," Layla said through her teeth. "There must be a place like the Gap nearby where I can get jeans that will fit and a shirt and shoes. And then you'll tell me what you're planning. You said you would."

He nodded. "Yes to both requests, *habiba*. In fact—let's go in here."

She blinked. This was not the Gap, this was a shop fronted with a heavy wooden door guarded by a major-domo dressed as a Cossack. The signature of a designer whose cheapest T-shirt would surely cost a king's ransom was scrawled in gold on the smoked-glass window.

"Here?"

"Here."

"Impossible. I can't—"

"You can," he said firmly, and led her past the smiling Cossack into the shop.

An acre of pale wood, glass shelves and discreet lighting stretched before them. The air was delicately perfumed with vanilla. A couple of fashionably dressed women moved from display to display; other women, tall and slender and almost frighteningly chic in severely cut black suits, hovered over them.

"*Madame. Monsieur*"

One of the black suits floated toward them. If she found anything unusual in Layla's outfit, she didn't show it.

Khalil smiled. "Do you speak English?"

"Yes, of course," the woman said, beaming at him.

He drew Layla forward. "We need a few things," he said pleasantly. "From top to bottom. Can you help us?"

Another bright smile. "But *certainement, monsieur.* It will be my pleasure. *Mademoiselle?* Will you come with me, please? *Monsieur?* You, too. We'll get you settled in and then I'll have coffee brought to you, *n'est-ce pas?*"

"No," Layla said desperately.

"Yes," Khalil said, and the sales clerk had no difficulty figuring out which of them had the final say.

Wasn't it Alice who'd gone through the looking glass?

This time it was Layla.

The clerk led them to an enormous room. Khalil settled into the corner of a white sofa that faced a curving wall of mirrors behind a raised, round platform. A very young woman, not wearing a black suit but a black dress, appeared as if by magic with a tray that held a carafe of coffee, cream, sugar and a translucent porcelain cup and saucer. A copy of the day's *International Herald Tribune* was already on the coffee table.

Layla was led past the mirrors to a room only slightly smaller than the one in which Khalil waited.

"If *mademoiselle* would kindly undress…"

The clerk held out a white dressing gown. Layla thought

of refusing it, of refusing to take off her clothes but she had the awful feeling the clerk would do whatever it took to make her follow the order. So she glared at the woman, even though it was the man waiting in the other room who deserved the glare, unlaced the clunky shoes and unzipped the jeans.

The clerk rewarded her with a beaming smile.

"Bien, mademoiselle," she said, and vanished through the door.

Layla was wrapped in the white dressing gown by the time she returned. And the parade of Gorgeous Stuff She Could Never, Ever Afford began.

Dresses. Blouses. Trousers. Jeans. Sweaters. Coats. Handbags and shoes and belts and, yes, underwear. Frothy thongs and lacy bras that made her want to sigh with wanting them.

There were no price tags on anything, but Layla wasn't fooled.

"Don't you have anything simpler?" she kept saying, meaning, "Don't you have anything I can afford?"

The clerk ignored her and, eventually, Layla gave up asking.

She was dressed, undressed, dressed, undressed. Six times. A dozen. And each new outfit meant she had to go out and stand on the round platform in front of all those mirrors.

In front of Khalil who sat, arms folded, looking like the potentate he was, nodding yes, no, shrugging his shoulders and occasionally offering a series of very unpotentatelike thumbs-ups.

And several very sexy, very masculine nods of approval.

Just having him looking at her that way was almost like having his hands on her. When she stepped on the platform in the final outfit, a long, slender column of silver silk and silver stiletto sandals, their eyes met. He rose, uncoiled from where he sat, came to her, ran his thumb lightly over her bottom lip and said, very softly, that she looked beautiful. Her knees almost buckled but she'd hung on to enough common sense to whisper that she couldn't afford anything she'd tried on.

"We will talk of it later, *habiba*."

"There's nothing to talk about!" She looked over her shoulder; the clerk smiled, then quickly looked away. "Do you have any idea what these things cost?"

"I have an excellent idea."

Yes, he probably did. He probably had mistresses by the dozen, women for whom he bought expensive gifts from places exactly like this, and why on earth should that put a little ache in her heart?

"Khalil," she said, struggling to sound reasonable, "it will take me years to repay you."

"These things are necessary if we are to carry out the rest of my plan."

"What's that supposed to mean?"

He smiled. "Patience, *habiba,* and you will find out."

"Do you ever listen to me?"

"Do *you* ever listen to *me?*" he said softly, and before she could stop him, he framed her face between his hands and brought her mouth to his for a swift, soft-as-air kiss. Then he turned to the clerk and handed her a card. "Send everything to me," he said.

Layla stared at him. Had he lost his mind?"

"*Mademoiselle* will wear the jeans she tried on minutes ago, the blue silk blouse and the leather jacket. And, of course, the blue leather stilettos."

"Of course, *monsieur.*"

"I would prefer the blouse in a deeper shade, if you have it."

"Khalil," Layla said.

"A shade closer to the color of *Mademoiselle*'s eyes," he added, with the imperious ease of a man who was, after all, king of the universe.

A man a woman could fall for, if she were dumb enough to let it happen.

Layla's head was filled with terrifying numbers as they left the shop, got into a taxi and headed back toward the river.

She loved what she was wearing—the low-cut jeans, the stiletto-heeled strappy sandals, the silk blouse in the exact shade of blue Khalil had demanded, the soft-as-butter leather jacket.

She would keep these things and return everything else. Even so, it would take her a century to pay off what she owed him.

And the bra and thong beneath it.

Oh, that bra. That thong. How easy it was to imagine herself wearing only those bits of silk and Khalil's dark head bent to her breasts, his powerful hands on her hips, then moving lower, pushing the thong aside, his fingers finding her, stroking her, oh God, tumbling her onto that huge bed so he could put his mouth where his fingers had been…

The cab pulled to the curb. Khalil stepped out, offered Layla his hand. She stumbled, blind to everything but the image in her mind.

He caught her around the waist and drew her to his side.

"Easy," he said softly. "I think we have to get some food into you, *habiba*."

She nodded. The thought of eating made her throat constrict, but it was safer to let him believe she was hungry than to admit the truth, even to herself, that she could not look at him without wanting him.

"I know a little café nearby." Khalil threaded his fingers through hers. "It's quiet and charming. I think you'll like it."

This was insane. He was behaving as if this were a normal day. And it wasn't. It wasn't. She was with him only because he came from a place where the twenty-first century didn't yet exist.

"It's just over there. And after, we can walk home over the *Pont Neuf*. That bridge, do you see? It's the oldest bridge in Paris."

Layla followed his pointing finger. The stone bridge stretched across the Seine, connecting the Right Bank to the Ile de la Cité.

"It's…it's very handsome," she said, trying to play the game as he was playing it, as if they were tourists.

Or lovers.

She swung toward him. It wasn't working. All this pretense on his part, that things were fine. The pretense on her part, that being with him wasn't affecting her…

"No," she said, a little breathlessly.

"No?"

He looked puzzled. She could hardly blame him. She'd gone along with it all until now.

"No, what?"

"No walks. No brunch. No anything until you tell me what happens next and when I can go home."

"*Habiba*. The café—"

"To hell with the café! Tell me now. Right now!"

Khalil's eyebrows rose. She was angry. Most women would have been smiling after a shopping trip—but Layla was not most women. Besides, he couldn't blame her for being angry. She had the right to know what came next and he'd put off telling her because he suspected she wouldn't like it.

Well, *he* didn't like it, either. Of course he didn't.

But there was no other way…

"Khalil? Damn it, answer me!"

They were almost at the café, a little place where the coffee and croissants were a taste of heaven, but, more important, a place where they could sit in a deep booth that would give them the privacy he'd need.

"All right, *habiba*. I'll tell you. But first—"

"No!" Layla stopped walking, slapped her hands on her hips and raised her flushed face to his. "You're going to tell me this minute. You're going to answer all my questions or I'll walk away from you, and to hell with your orders and threats. You got that?"

He got it. Only a fool wouldn't, he told himself, and took a deep breath.

"You must understand," he said carefully, "I have thought this through and there is no other way."

"No other way but what? How will you keep Omar and Butrus from turning what's happened into a bloody brawl? How will you convince your father you did the right thing? When do I go home and what part do I play in this grand scheme?"

Why was he looking at her like that? The morning was sunny and warm, but suddenly she felt chilled to the bone.

"A large part, *habiba*," he finally said. "A very large part. In fact, you might say yours will be the starring role."

His voice was low; his eyes had turned an icy gray. The passersby, the traffic, faded away. Layla's mouth felt as dry as the deserts of Al Ankhara.

"What starring role?" she whispered.

Khalil looked at her while an eternity seemed to slip by. Then he took her hands in his.

"You're going to marry me."

CHAPTER EIGHT

KHALIL had never proposed marriage in his life.

He'd never given any thought to it. It would happen someday; he'd assumed that. He was male, he was a sheikh, he was a prince who would eventually become sultan. He had obligations, commitments, and he knew it.

Someday he would take a wife and have children. There wasn't really any choice. Tradition and the continuance of his bloodline demanded it. He'd always known it would happen in the same sort of distant, uneasy way a healthy man knows he'll inevitably come down with a cold or the flu...

Well, he hadn't really proposed marriage now—he was going to explain that and quickly—but surely, when a woman heard words like the ones he'd just spoken, she said something to the man who'd spoken them.

Didn't she?

Layla hadn't said a word. She was staring at him, and the expression on her face was— What was the right way to describe it? Unsettling.

It was not what a man expected when he asked a woman to become his wife.

Though, of course, he had not really done that. When

it was time to marry, he'd do it the proper way. Confer with his father, discuss the necessary attributes a prince required in a wife. Together, they'd narrow the field to, say, half a dozen candidates. Candidates from Al Ankhara, naturally, or at least from The Nations.

This—his mention of marriage to Layla—had nothing to do with all that. He had no intention of actually marrying her. Hell, no. She was American, for one thing. She had a prickly personality, a streak of defiance a mile wide and an infuriating way of looking him straight in the eye, as if she were his equal.

Not that he didn't believe in equality of the sexes.

Okay. Maybe he didn't. A woman should understand her place in a man's life, especially if that man were going to someday rule his people. Walking one pace behind a man, even figuratively, was a Good Thing in a relationship, and why even think about such stuff?

He was not interested in marrying Layla.

The *announcement* of marriage to his father and to Omar was what was required in this situation. It was the only solution. Done properly, it would be enough to justify his having stolen her from Butrus.

Damn it, why didn't she say something? Why didn't she close her mouth? It had dropped open at the moment of his proposal—his pseudoproposal, and it had yet to shut.

The look on her face was beginning to make him angry.

Unless—for heaven's sake—unless she thought he really meant to marry her.

Khalil eased out a breath.

Of course. That was it. She'd taken his words at face value and she was still shocked by them. Shocked?

Hell, she was overcome.

Certainly she was. Yesterday she was to have been

Butrus's bride. Now, she was to be—correction—she *thought* she was to be the bride of a prince. Oh, she'd said a couple of things that made light of his title, but he hadn't put any credence in that.

Women loved titles. American women especially. How often had he and Tariq and Salim, both of them sheikhs and princes just as he was, talked about it? Well, Tariq was married now, and he'd admitted his wife hadn't given a damn about his title, but that was unusual.

Layla was clearly overcome.

Okay. He'd have to let her down easy. Her disappointment when she learned he had no intention of marrying her would be—

"Did you say…did you say, I would marry you?"

Khalil flashed a smile meant to assure her of his empathy. "I know how you must feel, *habiba,* but—"

"Marry you? Me?"

He narrowed his eyes. Was that sound she'd just made a snort? "Yes," he said through his teeth, with a growing awareness that his magnanimous offer was being met with something less than delight. "That is what I said."

Another snort. Hell, a guffaw! His jaw tightened. This was unacceptable. Inappropriate. It was downright insulting! And people were watching. Walking by, glancing at them with interest.

"Stop it," he growled.

"That's it. Snarl. That'll solve the whole problem."

Enough. He grabbed her elbow, jerked her around, saw a taxi and went toward it. Taxis didn't always stop in Paris; this one did because he literally stepped in front of it. The driver jammed on the brakes; Khalil stepped around it and jerked open the rear door.

"Get in," he said grimly.

"Why? So you can remind me that you all but own me? Is that a national pastime in your country?"

He could almost see the cabbie's ears rotating in their direction.

"Get in," he said grimly, and pushed her inside the cab. She scooted as far across the seat as she could. Khalil snapped out his address, and the taxi jerked into motion.

"I certainly got it right," Layla said bitterly. "From the frying pan straight into the fire!"

"I told you I had a plan. You said you wanted to hear it."

"And this—*this* is your plan? That I marry you? A man who's just like my father? Like Butrus?"

"I," he said coldly, "am not like anyone."

She laughed. He winced. He sounded like an idiot but it was her fault. She'd reduced him to behaving like one.

The taxi ground to a stop. They were caught in traffic. Khalil fumed. Tapped his fingers on his thigh. Then he cursed, dug out his wallet, tossed a bunch of Euros to the driver, opened the door and tugged Layla after him.

"Where are we going?"

"Where we can talk."

"Talk? You don't know the meaning of the word. You are exactly like the others. You are Omar and Butrus and your precious father rolled into one." She pulled away. He wrapped his hand around her wrist and she stumbled, thanks to the damned stiletto heels. "I'd sooner enter a convent!"

"No convent worth the name would grant you admittance."

"What's that supposed to mean?"

"Figure it out for yourself, and while you're doing it, walk faster."

"I can't walk faster. I don't want to walk faster. Who do you think you are? Forget that. I *know* who you are! You're a despot. A dictator. A—"

Enough, he thought in icy fury and, just as he had done once before, he slung her over his shoulder.

She shrieked. Beat her fists against his back.

"You cannot get away with this," she yelled. "This isn't Al Ankhara, it's Paris!"

And that was the problem.

Layla yelled. Khalil chuckled and called her his *petite chou,* his *chérie* as he strode past all the people out for a midmorning walk, and nobody tried to stop him.

Instead they laughed. They smiled. They called out encouragement. She was a woman, this was Paris, this was spring, and here was this good-looking man doing something incredibly romantic.

The doorman at his apartment building grinned and saluted. The concierge grinned and waved. Marianne was nowhere to be seen. She had undoubtedly gone shopping and a damned good thing she had, Khalil thought grimly, as he dropped both his smile and Layla.

He put her down on the white silk sofa in his enormous sitting room but she didn't stay there very long. She was on her feet in less than a second, throwing herself at him, claws extended like an enraged cat.

"You insufferable, egotistical, selfish son of a—"

He caught her hands, folded them within one of his. "Calm down."

"Calm down? *Calm* down? You...you carry me through the streets—"

"You wouldn't walk," he said reasonably.

"You announce that I'm going to marry you—"

"You demanded answers. Well, I'm trying to give you

some. To explain how we're going to get out of this situation."

Layla's eyes flashed with anger. "You keep calling it that. A situation. It isn't. It's—it's a nightmare."

Khalil let go of her hands, stepped back, folded his arms. She wanted answers? So did he.

"And how, exactly, did you end up in this nightmare? I think I'm entitled to the full story."

Tears rose in Layla's eyes. "Why do you do this? Why do you look at me as if I...as if I brought this down on my own head when *I'm* the one who was imprisoned, the one who was sold to a...to a monster by that pig, Omar."

He caught her wrist and tugged her toward him again and she gasped.

"That monster, as you call him, wanted to take you for his bride. And that pig is the man who gave you life."

"Omar took me prisoner and sold me to Butrus," she said bitterly. "Can't you get that through your head?"

"How did it happen? And why?" His jaw tightened. "How were you sold to Butrus? No one has given me the details."

Layla laughed. "What you mean is, you don't believe me."

"I believe you are Omar's daughter and that you were to be married to Butrus. I know nothing of the rest. I am thirty-two years old, *habiba*. I've never heard of things like this happening in my country, not in my lifetime, and suddenly all of it happened to you." His mouth twisted. "Don't you think that's unusual?"

"Maybe you never heard of them because you didn't want to hear of them!"

He wanted to tell her that was impossible, but was it? Could such things still go on in Al Ankhara? Had he done more than keep a physical distance from the place of his birth? Had he been keeping an intellectual distance from it, too?

Slowly he uncurled his fingers from her wrist. She stepped back and rubbed the bruised flesh.

"Tell me what happened," he said in a low voice. "All of it."

"I told you. I was kid—"

"All of it," he growled, "from the beginning."

It was the last thing she wanted to do. The details still horrified her, but the way Khalil was looking at her was horrifying, too. Did he think she'd invented this?

"What did your father tell you?" she asked, and watched his face.

He didn't answer immediately. The muscle that always seemed to flicker in his jaw when he was upset shifted into motion.

"He said you wanted to marry Butrus. That you wanted what it could bring you."

Layla wanted to laugh. Or maybe cry. Either way, it didn't matter. She was trapped in a world where men determined what was truth and what was not. Her mother had been trapped in that same place.

Well, to hell with that. She wasn't her mother and it was time she made that clear.

"In that case," she said with a cold smile, "why ask me anything? Obviously, you already have the answers."

That muscle danced again. He was angry, and wasn't that just too bad?

"I want to hear your explanation."

She looked at him, trying to read eyes that were unreadable. After a minute she shrugged her shoulders. She was tired of being the pawn that was to be sacrificed in a tough chess game.

A bad analogy. Or maybe a mixed metaphor. As if it mattered. She'd made a huge mistake. *That* was what mattered.

"Well?"

Layla lifted her chin, torn between telling him she didn't owe him an explanation and knowing that she did. No matter what she thought of this man, he had saved her life.

"Settle in for a long story," she said with a brashness she didn't feel.

And she told it to him.

All of it. Without any show of emotion, even though it still made her want to rage, to weep, to despise herself for ever having doubted her mother's version of events.

She described her childhood. How her mother waited tables in a succession of small New England towns, never staying longer than a few months in any one of them.

"Keeping a low profile, baby," she'd called it.

When Layla was ten, asking endless questions about the father she'd never known, her mother told her the truth.

Layla took a deep breath. "She was young. A struggling actress. She auditioned for a part in a film to be made in a place called Al Ankhara."

"A movie?" Khalil said, with obvious disbelief, "In my country? Not twenty-something years ago. It would have been impossible!"

"It was," Layla said, her mouth twisting. "She got the part, the producers sent her to Al Ankhara—and when she got there, she found out the ad and the film company were a front to lure women into the slave trade."

"Impossible," he said again, but with less conviction.

"Omar bought her. He…he used her. She became

pregnant and gave birth to me. Mama would say that having me was the only good thing that came out of what had happened to her." Layla's voice trembled. She looked away from Khalil, down at her hands, and saw that they were trembling, too. "But I didn't really believe her. It sounded preposterous, especially the stuff about the man who'd fathered me."

Khalil reached for her hands. They were shaking. He tugged her toward him and enfolded her fingers in his. It was what he'd done a little while ago, but this time he did it gently.

"Tell me the rest," he said softly. "All of it."

"She got away when he was on a trip. He'd given her some gold bracelets. She sold them and got us home, to America. Time went by. Mama began to believe Omar had forgotten about her. We stopped moving from town to town and settled in New York. She went from waitressing to managing a little place in Chelsea. I enrolled at New York University. I was going to study psychology, but—"

She paused. This was the hard part. Admitting to him, to herself, what a fool she'd been.

"Mama got sick. And…and after she was gone, I found myself thinking about the man who was my father." Her eyes met Khalil's. "How could he be such a monster? It just didn't seem possible."

"So you decided to come to Al Ankhara and find him."

"Not right away. I switched from psych to archaeology. Middle-Eastern archaeology. I can't explain it. I guess it had something to do with wanting to know more about myself. About my background." She swallowed dryly. "I took a quick course in Arabic. There was a guy in my class from this part of the world…"

"He taught you those useful phrases you tossed at me," Khalil said, trying to make her smile. It didn't work. Her lovely face remained white with tension.

"Yes. And then, I just decided to do it. Fly here. Find my father, Discover the parts of the story I was sure my mother had exaggerated."

"And?" Khalil said in a low voice.

"Omar pretended to be glad to see me. He invited me to stay at his home so we could get to know each other." She took a shaky breath. "He seemed so kind. So different from the man my mother had described…"

"But he wasn't," Khalil said grimly.

Layla shook her head. "Two days later, he said he had a surprise for me, that he had found me a husband. I said I didn't want a husband. I told him all the reasons I'd make a poor wife. He said they didn't matter. He told me to get dressed—that's when I found that all my own clothes were gone. He made me put on this…thing that made me look like a harem girl, then he had that monster with the knife force me downstairs and Butrus was waiting, and…and I ran away that night but Omar's men brought me back—"

Khalil cursed. He reached for her, wanting to gather her in his arms, kiss away the anguish in her eyes, but she shook her head wildly, jammed her hands against his chest and pushed him away.

"Don't."

"Layla. Sweetheart—"

"You're like the rest of them," she said bitterly. "You're like every man I've ever dealt with. You're all out to get what you want and to hell with anybody or anything else."

"I know how it seems, and I know I haven't been honest with you, that I probably should have told you everything I was going to do, but—"

"But you didn't. You thought that ordering me around, treating me as if I hadn't the intelligence to understand anything, would make me follow you blindly no matter what happened."

"No! Damn it, that's not true." It wasn't—was it? Khalil's jaw tightened. "I only did what was expedient."

"You mean, you did what would protect your father and his throne. Well, marrying you is *not* my idea of expedient, Your Highness. I am not my mother. I am not going to be—to be bought!"

"Layla." Khalil stepped back, raised his eyes to the ceiling, ran his hand through his hair. Damn it, how had he let things get to this point? "I'm not trying to buy you. The reason I said you'd have to marry me is—"

"I'm not stupid. I can figure it out." Her chin rose; her eyes glittered with accusation. "You're going to tell that precious council of your father's that you didn't give me to Butrus because *you* want me. Right?"

He cleared his throat. "Well, yes. It's the only solution, *habiba*. You see, I am the crown prince—"

"Are you ever!"

His eyes narrowed. "And what, precisely," he said, his voice suddenly low and dangerous, "does that mean?"

"You know damned well what it means. You're a prince. A sheikh. Heaven knows, you've reminded me of that often enough. You get whatever you want. And if you tell your father and those miserable old men that you want me, that you wanted me enough to…to kidnap me—"

"I did not kidnap you," he retorted.

"What do you call taking me to Paris, buying me things I could never afford and then announcing I'm going to marry you? Huh? What do you call that?"

"I call it utter nonsense," Khalil growled, grabbing her

by the shoulders. "The only part you have right is that the council, Omar, Butrus, even my father would have a difficult time denying me what I want. They'll all be angry—"

Layla snorted.

"All right. They'll be furious." His hands tightened on her. "But they'll have to go along with it." His mouth thinned. "Or would you rather I'd taken you to Kasmir and handed you over to your handsome bridegroom?"

"I'd rather you'd told me the truth, but then, why would you? I'm just a woman!"

Khalil glared at her. Damn it, she was impossible! All right. Maybe he should have told her everything, but it hadn't occurred to him. Okay. Maybe it had, but instinct had warned him she'd react exactly like this and he'd been pressed for time and what was the point?

It wasn't as if he'd needed her opinion. She had no choice; she had to go along with his plan. Why consult her when there were no alternatives?

"I'm just a woman," Layla said again, "and you're the emperor of the universe!"

He felt heat rise in his face.

He was not like that. He never thought of himself that way. He was only a man…

The hell he was.

He was what she'd said. A sheikh. A prince. And even though it galled him to consider the possibility—consider it, not acknowledge it, because he surely was not the arrogant, stiff-necked son of a bitch she was describing—

Or was he?

Damn it, he didn't need this. Not now. He had power. Fine. And this was the time to use it, not the time to permit a fast-talking female to turn him into a guy lying on a shrink's couch.

She had forgotten that she was still in danger. If his ploy didn't work, if Omar decided to come after what he thought of as his property... Hell, if things had moved more swiftly than he'd anticipated and Omar or Butrus were already on their trail...

Khalil drew a deep breath. He was the only man who could save her. Was he also the only man who could make her melt in his arms when he kissed her?

And that was the way to deal with her. It was the only way.

He pulled her hard against him. She struggled; he captured her face between his hands and kissed her.

She didn't respond.

He kissed her again, hard and deep.

She stood still within his embrace, an unmoving as a statue.

A shudder went through him. He dropped his hands to his sides and took a step back.

"I'm going out," he said tonelessly.

She was weeping, but in silence, her arms wrapped around herself as if she were cold straight through to the marrow of her bones.

"When I return, we'll discuss what we must do next."

That brought back a spark of life. "I know what *I'm* doing next!"

"Leave? Run away? Go to your embassy?" He smiled thinly, hurting deep inside and not knowing why, knowing only that wounding her might rid him of the hurt. "You have no money. No passport. Not that having either would change things for you, *habiba*. I am, as you so helpfully pointed out, a sheikh. A prince. The heir to an ancient throne. Do you really think your government would involve itself in a lovers' quarrel?"

"That's not what this is!"

"No?" Another thin smile. "That's what I'll call it, and who do you think they'd believe? A hysterical woman who can't prove her identity, or me?" His smile vanished. "Then there's the very real possibility that Omar's and Butrus's men are already prowling the streets, searching for you."

Her face paled. "How could they know I'm here?"

"Money buys information. It is the first thing one learns when one is king of the universe." Khalil went to the door. "If you value your life, you will stay here."

She would. There were security service operatives watching the front and back entrances of the building. He'd set that in motion with a phone call. One man had even followed them at a discreet distance when they went shopping this morning.

He would protect her, even if she hated him for it. He had to keep her safe. For his father. For the throne.

For himself.

"I'll never marry you," she said, her voice trembling.

His hand was on the doorknob. All he had to do was tell her he had no intention of marrying her.

But he didn't.

He went back to her instead, threaded his hands into her hair and kissed her again. It was the kiss of a man who always gets what he wants.

The kiss of a conqueror.

The kiss of a man walking a tightrope and not wanting to face the real reason for it.

Khalil turned, went out the door and into the bright Paris afternoon.

CHAPTER NINE

IN LATE afternoon the sun began playing peek-a-boo with a towering bank of clouds.

Eventually, the clouds swallowed the sun and rain poured onto the city. The gutters foamed with raging torrents of water; people scurried for shelter.

Khalil put up his jacket collar, jammed his hands in his pockets and kept walking.

What was a little rain when a man was hot with fury?

He'd been walking for hours. Along the Seine. The Champs Elysées. Across the Champs de Mars and along narrow streets that led nowhere. He'd stood on the Pont Neuf and stared down at the murky water, and none of that had done a damned thing to defuse his anger.

So, yeah, why not try a soaking shower with your clothes on?

Who did Layla Addison think she was? He'd saved her neck and she thanked him by insulting him! The woman had called him names, laughed in his face and reacted to his proposal of marriage as if he were the bogeyman.

A truck rumbled by, its tires sending a spray of water over the curb and over Khalil's legs. His head came up; he flashed the driver the kind of look Layla deserved.

To hell with her.

He should have kept out of it. Let her be dragged away and handed over to Butrus. Who gave a damn? Okay, he did, but only because of the damage something like that would have done to his father.

Another truck. Another wave of water. Khalil snarled as the vehicle shot by.

He'd done this for his father, not the woman, and—

"Khalil?"

Never for the woman. Why would he take such risks for—

A hand fell on his arm. He jerked back, glared at the stranger who'd dared to intrude on his dark thoughts...and blinked with astonishment.

"Salim?"

The tall, dark-haired man grinned. "The one and only."

"Salim!" Khalil smiled. The men shook hands, then turned the handshake into a quick bear hug. "What are you doing in Paris?"

"I have offices here, remember?" Sheikh Salim al Taj, Crown Prince of the Kingdom of Senahdar, drew back and gave Khalil an assessing look. "You waiting for a life raft or what?"

For the first time in hours, in what felt like a lifetime, Khalil laughed.

"Or what," he said, and clapped Salim on the back. "To hell with the life raft. How about a brandy?"

"I don't care what anybody says," Salim said, straight-faced. "The rumor that you have a brain is true."

Laughing, the men headed for a bar.

They took a table near a fireplace, ordered Napoleon brandy and fell into the kind of easy conversation that came of knowing each other since they were eighteen.

There was a lot to talk about; they hadn't seen each other in a while.

Still, Khalil's thoughts drifted. What was Layla doing while he sat here, talking with Salim?

"...dinner with Tariq. He mentioned some property in Colorado... Spectacular, he says."

He had never been as angry with anyone as he was with her. Damn it, he'd saved her from Butrus. Didn't that at least rate a thank-you?

"...suggested the three of us might want to go into this together. Buy the property, build three ski lodges..."

Okay, she didn't know his offer of marriage hadn't been real, that he'd only meant they'd have to pretend they were planning on marriage, but suppose he'd meant it? She'd acted as if becoming his wife was the worst thing possible.

"...all fly there, check things out. Khalil? What do you think?"

Khalil blinked. Focused on Salim, who was obviously waiting for him to speak.

"Uh, what do I think about...?"

"About buying land in Colorado."

Buying land? Khalil stalled for time. "Oh, that."

"Yes. 'That.' Do you like the idea?"

"Well, it sounds, ah, it sounds interesting. You have anything specific in mind?"

Salim rolled his eyes. "Land in Colorado. The three of us, together." He sighed. "You haven't heard a word I said, have you?"

"Sorry. I was just..." Khali let out a long breath. "I have things on my mind. Business. You know."

"Bull," Salim said, and signaled for refills. "It's a woman."

"The hell it is!"

"What's her name?"

"I just told you, there is no..." The barman set fresh brandies before them. Khalil lifted his, swirled it, took a hefty swallow. "Okay. You're right, and you're wrong. This involves a woman but not the way you think."

"There's only one right way to think when it comes to women," Salim said a little grimly. "With your head instead of your— Hell. Never mind. Talk to me, man. What's going on?"

Talk? What good would that do? This wasn't Harvard, where three eighteen-year-old Arab princes had often sat up half the night, talking about feeling lost in a strange, exciting land called America.

No. It wasn't. Still, maybe talking would help. Maybe he could figure out how he'd managed to turn a mess into a disaster.

He looked up, met Salim's eyes and nodded. "I went home last week," he said slowly, "and I walked into one hell of a situation."

They ordered food and a bottle of Burgundy wine to replace the brandy.

Khalil talked and talked, then fell silent. Salim cleared his throat.

"So, bottom line, you decided you had to keep your father from making a terrible mistake so you violated his trust, upset his council, stole another man's bride and now you have to convince her to marry you."

So much for Salim's help.

"No," Khalil said coldly, "that is not the bottom line."

"Look, I understand. You did the only thing you could. I'd have done the same. Still, those are the facts."

They were, and why try to deny it?

"More or less," Khalil said glumly. "Except the marriage part. I won't marry her, I just need my father to think I will. By Ishtar, why would I? A woman I hardly know. An American, well, raised in America, with no concept of what it is to be the wife of a sheikh."

"And you left a note for your father with Hassan."

"Yes." Khalil pulled back his sleeve, glanced at his watch. "He's delivered it by now."

"And the note says…"

"That I regretted I could not honor his command but that I desired the woman for myself. I figure I'll give it a week, call my father, tell him I went a little crazy, made Layla my mistress, not my wife—"

"Another lie?"

"Yes. Of course. Two lies, in fact. I have no intention of—"

"Take it easy. I'm just trying to put it all together. So, in the end, you save your father's exalted royal ass— pardon me for being blunt, but that's the truth. Omar gets the satisfaction of assuming his daughter is the prince's mistress, and the bridegroom…?"

"He gets a small fortune in gold." Khalil gave a thin smile. "And my personal promise of what will happen to him, should he ever make trouble again."

"Well, it sounds fine. And you've stashed the woman at your place?"

Khalil nodded.

"You're sure she won't bolt?"

"She's not stupid. She has no passport, no money, and I made sure she knows that Butrus won't be happy."

"The groom?"

"Yes."

"Wouldn't that be an understatement? I assume the man could be a real danger."

"You assume correctly," Khalil said, his tone harsh. "I arranged for round-the-clock bodyguards to watch the building. Front entrance, rear entrance…" The muscle in his jaw knotted. "I've phoned them every hour. They haven't spotted anyone suspicious but I won't relax until this thing is over."

"You're worried about the woman," Salim said softly.

"I'm worried about my father and the throne," Khalil said…and then he let out a long breath. "Hell, yes, I'm worried about her. Why wouldn't I be?" he added gruffly. "She didn't ask for any of this to happen."

Salim held up his hands. "Easy, my friend. No need to be defensive."

"I am not being…" Another long breath. "Sorry. It's been a rough few days."

"Just one question. How come you didn't tell her the proposal wasn't real?"

"She didn't give me the chance. I said she had to marry me, she said no." He shrugged. "And I walked out."

"Understandable. A woman turns down a man's offer of marriage…"

"Damn it, what did I just tell you? I did not offer her marriage!"

"She thinks you did."

"Yes, but…"

Yes, but so what? Where was it written Layla had to fling herself into his arms if he proposed to her? It was a good thing she hadn't. The situation would be even more touchy.

"You're having an ego problem," Salim said.

"Ridiculous! I am not…" Khalil sighed. "Maybe."

"Forget maybe. You just can't believe she didn't jump at the chance to become your ever-loving bride."

Silence, then another shrug. "I guess that's possible."

Salim grinned. "It's more than possible. It's a fact. And who could blame you? Aside from me, you're the best catch there is."

Khalil gave what might have been a real smile. "Thank you, I think."

"All you have to do is go home, tell her the marriage thing is just a scam, she says, 'Oh, in that case, I'm fine with it.' Problem solved."

Khalil's smile broadened. "Thank you, Dear Abby."

"My pleasure. Now, how about a little celebration? I found this great jazz club in Montmartre—"

"Let me take a rain check, okay? I need to deal with this right away."

The men rose. Khalil dropped a handful of Euros on the table, they shook hands and promised to keep in touch.

Then Salim sat down, his smile fading.

Khalil was lucky. He'd had a problem with a woman and they'd just solved it. That was the way things ought to be.

How come they rarely were?

By the time his taxi pulled to the curb, Khalil was feeling pretty good.

Problem solved, just as Salim had said. Why he'd been riled by Layla's reaction to his proposal—his phony proposal—was beyond him. The stress of the last few days, perhaps. Whatever the reason, it was history.

Layla probably wouldn't want to talk to him, but that was fine. She didn't have to. He'd do all the talking, sort this thing out, then phone his father.

Definitely, problem solved.

It had started to rain again. An understatement. The late-evening sky had gone black and as he stepped from the cab, a bolt of lightning, accompanied by a roar of thunder, swept down from the heavens.

Khalil dashed across the sidewalk just as the doorman hurried toward him, umbrella unfurled.

"Bon soir, monsieur le sheikh."

"Hello, Jean. Hell of a night, isn't it?"

The doorman chuckled. "That is exactly what I said to the *mademoiselle* when she went out earlier. Well, not in those very words, *certainement,* but—"

Khalil stood still. "Mademoiselle?" he said carefully. "You mean, the young lady who is staying with me?"

"Oui."

Khalil felt a sudden tightness in his chest. "You must be mistaken. She couldn't have gone out."

The doorman's smile faltered. "But she did, sir. I recognized her immediately. Not just by her face—she is very beautiful—but by what she wore. Another, ah, another eccentric outfit, *non?* Men's clothes, as it were…"

Khalil punched the door open, ran past the startled concierge at the desk, jabbed at the elevator's call button, cursed when he saw the floor indicator and made a detour to the service stairs. He pounded up the flights, opened the door to his apartment…

"Layla! Layla, where are you?"

No answer.

"Marianne? Damn it, answer me!"

He ran through the enormous rooms. No Layla. No Marianne, only a note in the kitchen explaining that her son had called, he had to work tonight and so did his wife. She was sorry but she had to leave to care for her two little grandchildren.

Khalil dropped the note. He ran his hands through his wet hair.

"Layla." He spoke in a whisper but her name seemed to echo through the apartment. "Layla," he said again, waiting for a rush of anger to overtake him, a reaction that would have been a thousand times preferable to the cold twist of terror in his gut.

Where could she have gone? Why hadn't the men watching the building stopped her?

He pulled out his cell phone, called the numbers for the men on guard. He hadn't noticed anyone outside the building. Maybe they had left early…

They hadn't.

Two men were in a van across from the front entrance. Two others were in the narrow alley in back. None had seen a woman answering Layla's description. They hadn't seen anyone. Well, nobody but him. And, oh yeah, a boy in jeans and a cap.

Khalil slammed the phone shut. He was trembling with anger.

What good were detectives who couldn't tell a boy from a woman? And what kind of irresponsible, ungrateful creature was Layla to have left him?

Didn't she understand what he'd sacrificed for her?

His heart rose into his throat.

Didn't she know what it would do to him if something happened to her?

Layla hadn't left him. *He* had left *her.* Alone, penniless, with nothing but fear and his housekeeper for company. Now she was alone in the night, in the rain, on the streets of a strange city…

And, for all he knew, with Butrus's thugs in hot pursuit.

Khalil groaned with despair.

He was everything she'd said he was, selfish, arrogant and someone who'd abandoned her to make her suffer. To make her pay for having said no to his proposal. To hurt her as she had hurt him by not wanting him because he wanted her, God, he wanted her, in his arms, in his bed—

He was wasting time.

He ran. Out the door, down the stairs, through the lobby. The concierge called after him as he flew past. So did the doorman. Was something wrong? Could they help?

No one could help. This was his fault and only he could remedy it. If he didn't find Layla… No. An idea like that was an admission of defeat.

"Think," he muttered as he looked up, then down the wet, deserted streets.

Where would she go? A café, even though she hadn't the money to buy anything? The Métro station? An unfriendly place at night but maybe she'd figured she could, at least, keep dry. Or…or had she slipped from the building and straight into the vile embrace of her would-be groom or one of his men.…

Khalil kept a car here, a Lamborghini that he garaged a couple of blocks away. He ran to the building, got into the car and gunned the engine. The tires skidded a little as he turned onto a rain-slicked, cobblestone street, but he fought for control, got it and stepped down on the gas pedal.

The car shot forward.

In a way the rain and the night simplified things.

He could drive fast because the streets were all but empty. He could spot the few pedestrians when he was a block away. Plenty of time to slow down and check them in the bright glare of his headlights, then roar away again.

He saw dog walkers. Lovers. Tourists, too stupid or too excited to care about the weather. The good news was that he didn't see Omar or Butrus…

The terrifying news was that he didn't see Layla, even

after he'd driven all the streets of the Ile de la Cité. Now, it was decision time.

Khalil pulled to the curb.

The Pont Neuf was just ahead, spanning the black waters of the Seine. If he took it he'd end up on the Left Bank.

Paris was a huge city. If his Layla were on the run, which part of the city had she chosen?

Khalil grasped the steering wheel with both hands and refused to think about looking for the proverbial needle in a haystack. Instead, he tried to put himself in her mind. Would she have chosen the Left or the Right Bank? They'd been there today. She might feel those streets held some familiarity…

The hair on the nape of his neck rose.

Someone was standing on the bridge.

A boy? Maybe. Medium height. Slender build. A boy, yes—except, what kid would stand staring out over the Seine with the rain beating down on his head, the wind whipping at him so hard it tore off his cap and a glorious mane of golden hair flew out behind him?

Slowly Khalil stepped out of the Lamborghini. He said Layla's name.

She spun toward him.

"Layla," he said again.

Heart hammering, he began to run even though time was moving in slow motion. He couldn't seem to gain ground despite his pounding footsteps….

And then, suddenly, he was there. On the bridge, only inches from his Layla, the uncaring black water of the Seine flowing below.

"Layla," he whispered, "sweetheart, please forgive me. I'm sorry. I was wrong. I was wrong, *habiba*…"

"Khalil," Layla sobbed, and flung herself into his arms.

CHAPTER TEN

KHALIL pulled the Lamborghini to the curb in front of his apartment building.

He got out of the car, opened the passenger door and scooped Layla into his arms.

"I can walk," she said, even as she wrapped her arms around his neck.

"I know you can, *habiba*. But I want to carry you."

She buried her face against his throat. He could feel the moist warmth of her breath against his skin as he entered the lobby. Both the doorman and the concierge reacted to the sight of the owner of the penthouse carrying a woman in his arms with admirable restraint.

"My car is out front." Khalil tossed the keys to the concierge. "Take care of it."

He knew he sounded abrupt, but all he could think of was how close he'd come to losing his Layla. Nothing else mattered.

The night wrapped around them in a velvet embrace when he stepped inside his apartment. He elbowed the door shut and stood without moving. It was safe to put her down, but he didn't. He couldn't.

Holding her seemed the most important thing in the world.

Raindrops glittered in her hair. Her shirt—his shirt, he thought with a strange rush of warmth—was wet. She looked bedraggled and half-drowned and—

And absolutely beautiful.

He knew what to do next. You didn't have to be a Boy Scout to figure it out. He had to get her warm and dry. That meant a hot shower. A soft, thick robe. A fire on the hearth, a snifter of cognac…

Slowly, Layla raised her head and looked at him.

"Khalil," she whispered.

"Yes, *habiba,*" he whispered in return, and kissed her.

It was a gentle kiss, only the soft touch of his lips against hers. She made a little sound, something between a moan and a sigh. Her hand rose, cupped the back of his head. What could a man do except bend his head and take her lips again?

And again.

A longer kiss. A deeper one. A kiss that made her lips soften and cling to his.

Khalil groaned.

He was sure he knew what was happening. She'd run away on the spur of the moment and he'd found her just as she began regretting what she'd done. She was grateful to him; he had saved her from the night, from the rain, from possible harm.

He could take what he wanted. She would not stop him.

But he wanted more.

He wanted her to trace the outline of his lips with her fingertip. Yes, like that. To smile into his eyes. Yes, just like that. To look at him the way a woman looks at a man when she desires him.

It took all his self-control to catch her hand in his and press a kiss into her palm.

"Layla. *Habiba.* I understand. You've gone through a bad time. It's…it's natural that you should turn to me for—"

She kissed him. He fought against sinking into the kiss, forced himself to take his lips from hers and speak calmly.

"Sweetheart, you'll regret this. When you have time to think—"

"I *have* thought," she whispered. "For hours. I thought about what a fool I'd been to drive you away."

"You didn't. I was the one who—"

She silenced him with another kiss, her mouth open against his, her teeth sinking delicately into his lip.

And he was lost.

Her hunger set him on fire. His arms tightened around her. His mouth bore down on hers, his tongue seeking hers as he carried her through the silent, high-ceilinged apartment.

"Khalil," she said, and the urgency in her voice told him his bedroom was much too far away.

Halfway there, blood pounding, heart racing, he whispered words that made her tremble with desire as he lowered her to her feet. She lifted herself to him, nipped at his mouth and began pushing his jacket from his shoulders.

He tore it off. Tore off his shirt. Began undoing the buttons on her shirt, but his fingers didn't seem to be working right. A button popped; Layla gave a low, wicked laugh and it drove him into even greater frenzy.

Growling, he tore the shirt open and slid it back on her shoulders, trapping her arms. She was naked, her breasts round and rose-tipped. Her scent rose to his nostrils, rain and night, vanilla and honey.

And Layla. The essence that was hers alone.

"Beautiful," he said thickly, but she was more than that. She was proud and strong and brave, and his need for her surpassed anything he'd ever known.

Slowly he lifted his hands and cupped her breasts. She sighed; her eyes went wide and dark.

"Do you want me, *habiba?*" His voice was low and hot with passion. "Do you want me?" he said again.

She answered by bringing his head to her breasts. Need flashed through him, building until he was almost blind with pleasure. He sucked first one delicate nipple and then the other, and Layla's cry of ecstasy rose into the night.

It was the most exciting sound he had ever heard, the sound he had waited for his entire life.

The last of his control shattered.

He ripped off the rest of her clothes. Tore open his belt. Yanked down the zipper of his jeans and kicked them away. Lifted Layla in his arms and backed her against the wall. Her legs wrapped around him. He cupped her bottom, and with one hard, deep thrust, claimed her as his.

"Khalil," she said brokenly, "Khalil, Khalil…"

He plunged deep, again and again, loving the feel of her. She was tight and wet and hot, riding him with her head thrown back, sobbing, pleading for him to end the exquisite torture, but he gritted his teeth and held back, held back, held back because this—the woman in his arms, her heat, her cries, her taste—marked the beginning and end of the universe.

And then, at last, it was too much. There was no choice but to let go, let go, to shudder with ecstasy and expel his essence deep into her womb.

She cried out again. Her muscles contracted around him, and he let go of all that he was and made Layla his.

* * *

Minutes passed, or perhaps an eternity.

Khalil groaned. Could he move? He wasn't sure.

Layla was still wrapped around him. They were plastered together, torso to torso, bodies slick with sweat. His legs were rubber; the breath rasped in his throat.

She sighed. Her hair brushed against his lips as she turned her head and kissed his throat.

"*Habiba?* Are you all right?"

"Mmm."

"Is that a yes?"

"Mmm."

He smiled, his lips against her temple.

"Khalil? I think you have to put me down."

She was right. It was the only way to find out if either of them could stand without the support of the other.

"I know." He pressed his forehead to hers. "I'm just not sure who's holding who upright, so anything might happen when I do."

Her laugh was soft, sexy and knowing.

"But it's worth the risk," she whispered, "don't you think? Otherwise, Marianne's going to be in for a big shock tomorrow morning."

The picture she'd drawn made him grin. His very staid, very proper housekeeper had already had enough shock.

"Okay," he said solemnly. "For Marianne's sake, then."

Slowly he eased Layla to her feet, but he kept his arms around her. The truth was, he couldn't imagine ever letting go of her.

"Good," he said. "We're both still standing."

Layla smiled, then blushed. "Don't look at me that way."

"What way?" She was so beautiful. So incredibly lovely. And he—was it possible? He already wanted her again. "What way, *habiba?*" he said, between gentle, nibbling kisses.

Female, flustered, she lifted a hand to her hair. "I'm a mess."

"You're perfect," he said softly, and gave her a much longer kiss.

Her lips curved against his. "Liar."

"Me?" He drew back, did his best to look indignant. "Don't you know that princes never lie?"

Just as he'd hoped, she gave another of those sweet laughs.

"What you mean is that princes are always diplomatic." She smiled. "You're that. And you're also easy on the eyes, Lord Khalil."

Right. He knew how he must look. His hair, wet and standing up in little tufts. His jaw, shadowed by his end-of-day beard.

"Yeah, well, rain and wind will do that."

Her smile tilted, if only a little. "All because of me."

"I'm just grateful I found you, sweetheart."

"Me, too." Her voice was small, muffled as she leaned closer and laid her head against his chest. His arms tightened around her. "You've been so good to me, Khalil. And I repaid you by running away."

"Stop!" He knew he'd spoken more harshly than he'd intended but he couldn't help it. He pressed a kiss to her hair. "I don't want your gratitude. God knows, I certainly don't deserve it."

"Yes, you do! If you hadn't risked everything to save me, by now I'd be—"

"Hush, sweetheart. Don't think about him. Butrus is history."

"What will he do to you?" she said, raising her head and looking into his eyes. "Something, Khalil. I know that. A beast like Butrus won't simply accept losing something he—something he believes belongs to him."

"He'll have to," he said with deliberate lightness. "I'm the king of the universe, remember?"

Layla smiled. "And modest, too."

He smiled back at her. Then his smile dimmed. He framed her face between his hands.

"I was frantic when I realized you were gone, *habiba*. All I could think about was you, alone in Paris, and that it was my fault."

"It wasn't."

"It was. I should have explained what I was planning." His jaw tightened. "Calling me king of the universe wasn't actually a mistake, sweetheart. I'm not proud of it but the truth is, I'm not accustomed to explaining myself to anyone."

"But you just did," Layla said softly. "Thank you for that."

Khalil smoothed her tousled hair back from her face.

"I'll tell you what I'm planning, and you tell me if you're willing to go along with it. Okay?"

She nodded.

"But first…" He tipped up her chin and kissed her. "First, though, let me do what I should already have done. Run you a hot bath. Make you a warm drink." He gathered her close in his arms. "I want to take care of you, *habiba*. Please, will you let me?"

Layla smiled. Only a foolish woman would not have said yes.

And only an even more foolish one would have let her heart flood with an emotion too frightening to admit.

Khalil had meant every word.

He made her a mug of hot chocolate. While she drank it, he filled the enormous tub in his bathroom with hot water, added scented oil—sandalwood, she thought—turned on the jets and then carried her into it. There was a skylight above the tub; the rain and clouds had been swept away and a billion stars blazed above them.

"Good?" he said.

"Wonderful," Layla sighed.

"Here. Turn around. That's it. Now scoot back."

She did, and he drew her between his legs. She sank against him, eyes closed, luxuriating in the scent of the water and the feel of his body. Was it possible to go from terror one day to joy the next?

She felt his hands in her hair, gently massaging her scalp. Washing away the rain, the night, the fear.

Another deep sigh. "Lovely," she whispered.

His hands drifted lower. He washed her body with slow, gentle strokes of his soapy hands. Very efficiently at first. And then with growing deliberation.

His hands lingered on her breasts. Teased the nipples till they were erect. Slid down over her belly and cupped her tenderly. She threw her head back against his shoulder.

He could see the passion in her face as he put his lips to her ear.

"Open for me," he said thickly. "Open for me, *habiba*."

She did, parting her thighs, crying out as he slid his hand between them.

"Khalil…"

His thumb slid over her clitoris. His other hand cupped her breast, played with the budded nipple. She heard herself making desperate sobs of pleasure, felt his heart racing beneath her ear…

Felt the silken pressure of his engorged penis seeking entrance, the tip easing inside her. She gasped at the slow, exquisite penetration. He drew back, then entered her ever so slightly again.

It wasn't enough. It would never be enough. She needed—she needed—

"Tell me," he whispered. "Tell me what you want."

Him. Only him, for ever and ever and ever.

"Tell me," he said roughly, but she couldn't. Needing him, wanting him, was terrifying. She couldn't give in to it, couldn't, couldn't...

He teased her again, sliding in, pulling back, sliding in. A whimper of frustration rose in her throat.

"You," she said, "only you. Please, Khalil, please..."

He growled her name. Turned her in his arms. Brought her down on his rigid length.

And Layla shattered into a million bits of starlight.

Afterward they showered together. Dried off with thick, soft towels. Slipped into Khalil's huge bed. He drew the duvet over them, then gathered her close.

Layla was very quiet.

Did she regret what they'd just done?

She had lived a nightmare for days. He had made things even worse, behaving as he had this afternoon. And what had he done to soothe her?

He'd made love to her, first against a wall. He smothered a groan of despair—a wall! Then he'd made love to her again, in the tub when it should have been here, in the cocooning softness of his bed, with candles lighting the room.

Had he hurt her?

He'd been rough and quick and she...she'd been so tight, so tight as he penetrated her, as she closed around him...

And, idiot that he was, if he kept thinking this way, he

was going to give himself a hard-on. There were, after all, some things best described in American English.

"Layla," he whispered. "*Habiba,* did I hurt you?"

"Did you…?" She put her palm against his cheek. "No. Oh, no, you didn't hurt me."

"*Saamihnii.* Forgive me, *habiba.* I should not have made love to you this way. So quickly. So roughly—"

"It wasn't quick or rough. It was…it was—"

"Wonderful," he said softly, because it had been, wonderful beyond belief, and because now he saw what he'd hoped to see in her eyes.

More than wonderful, Layla thought. That was why she'd gone quiet. She'd been with one other man. She knew what the aftermath of sex was supposed to be like; at least, she'd thought she did.

But this, what she felt now, in Khalil's arms…

"*Habiba.* Tell me the truth. If I hurt you—"

Layla put her fingers gently over his mouth. Teasing him was better than confronting the emotions rushing through her.

"Are you looking for compliments, my king of the universe?"

Khalil flashed the kind of arrogant grin that would have made her hiss with anger a couple of days ago.

"A man is a fool to turn them away, especially when they are from a beautiful woman, *habiba.*"

"Is that an old Al Ankharan saying?"

Another of those cocky grins. Did he know he was the most gorgeous man in the world? That his strength was matched only by his tenderness? He'd said he didn't want her gratitude. What would he say if he knew that what he had was her—was her—

"If it isn't," he said, between light kisses, "it should be."

He laughed, as did she. His kisses grew deeper. He could feel the drugging heat of desire thickening his blood. How could it be? He not only wanted her again, he was ready to take her again.

No. He was a man, not a beast. He had promised to care for her, and even though it had taken him a while to get around to it, he would.

He gave her one last kiss, then settled her against him. She snuggled closer. After a minute he touched the tip of her nose with his finger.

"*Habiba,* I'm famished. How about if I make us something to eat?"

"S'a fine idea."

"A sandwich? Scrambled eggs? Layla?"

Her lashes drifted to her cheeks. Her breathing slowed. Khalil kissed her forehead. Then he, the man who never took a woman to his bed for anything but sex, gathered his Layla against him, tucked her head on his shoulder and followed her into sleep.

He woke to early-morning sunlight and an empty space beside him.

The awful hollowness of fear gripped his belly.

"Layla?"

No. She couldn't have left him. Not after last night.

He sprang from the bed, pulled on a pair of jeans, hurried out of the bedroom—and heard the faint sound of music and smelled the rich aroma of fresh coffee coming from the kitchen.

It couldn't be Marianne. She always turned on the radio in the morning but only to hear the news; she never used it to play music. Besides, this was her late day; she wouldn't be in until afternoon.

Barefoot, silent, Khalil made his way to the kitchen and saw Layla, filling the French press with boiling water. She wore one of his shirts—she did much more for them than he ever had—and her golden hair spilled down her back as she moved her hips in time to Norah Jones's sultry voice.

His heart seemed to swell.

"Hey," he said softly.

She swung toward him. A smile lit her face. He went to her, took her in his arms and kissed her.

"Good morning, *habiba*."

"Good morning."

"Did you sleep well?"

A rosy glow lit her face. "Very well. And you?"

Khalil grinned. "I slept like a rock." He kissed her, slowly and tenderly. "So," he said teasingly, "I see that making coffee is another of your talents."

She laughed. "So are waffles. Or pancakes. Or scrambled eggs. Your choice."

"Mmm." Another kiss. "Absolutely my choice?"

She blushed again. He loved that sweep of color.

"Breakfast," she said firmly, putting her hands against his chest. "And make yourself useful. Set the table. Get out the eggs and the milk." He chuckled as she turned away. She swung back, saw him grinning. "What?"

"Nothing," he said with absolute innocence. What would she say if he told her no one had ever before ordered him to do anything?

Layla lifted her eyebrows. "Do you even know how to set a table, king of the universe?"

"Of course," he said.

He was a grown man. How hard could it be? Not hard at all, as it turned out.

Plates. Silverware. Napkins, though he had to search to

find them. And then pancakes and hot coffee and Layla, smiling at him across the table.

In the midst of it all, he had a sudden realization.

He was happy.

Surely he'd been happy before?

This couldn't be the first time the sun had seemed so bright, the breeze coming through the window so soft, the food he ate so delicious. It couldn't be the first time he'd watched a woman's face and wanted to rise from his chair, take her in his arms, kiss her and tell her—

"Khalil? What's wrong?"

He cleared his throat. "Nothing, sweetheart. Everything is—"

"Perfect," she said softly. "Unbelievably perfect."

He nodded. It was. There was no other word to describe the night and now the morning. He pushed back his chair and got to his feet.

"Layla."

Her eyes darkened. He went to her, held out his hand and she let him pull her gently to her feet. She lifted herself to him and pressed her mouth to his. Coffee and maple syrup and the taste that was hers alone filled his senses.

"Layla." His voice was low. "Sweetheart. I promised you an explanation."

"Yes," she whispered, and kissed him again.

"About what comes next. About my proposal of marriage."

Another kiss. Khalil stopped thinking and led her to the bedroom where they tumbled into the bed together.

Explanations could wait.

What he wanted now was to kiss all the shadowed places he had not explored before. To run his hand lightly down Layla's body, cup her breast, watch her face as he teased the nipple, kissed her belly, her thighs, parted the sweet folds between them so he could taste the feminine bud he found there.

He loved this. Her scent. Her heat. Her cries as he brought her to climax with his fingers, his tongue, his mouth.

At last, when he could wait no longer, when she was begging for his possession, he slid deep inside her. Moved. Moved again. Layla began to tremble. Her hands clutched at his biceps. She moaned.

"Let go," he said. "Let go, sweetheart. Let me see it happen."

A shudder tore through her. She sobbed his name; her body arched like a bow and as it did, Khalil threw back his head and followed her into oblivion.

A long time later he stirred. He was lying over her, his weight pinning her to the mattress. He shifted away, loving her murmured protest, and drew her close to him. She sighed, put her head on his shoulder, draped a leg over his.

It was time to tell her what he'd planned. The call to his father. News of a proposed marriage that would, of course, not take place.

Layla sighed again. Her warm breath tickled his damp throat. Amazing. He had spent the night with her in his arms. Now she was there again. Amazing, indeed, for a man who'd never spent a whole night with a woman in any bed, his or hers.

Why would he? Any man with half a brain knew where that kind of foolishness could lead. Her lipstick in his bathroom. His toothbrush in hers. Expectations, familiarity and then, indubitably, inevitably, boredom.

No way.

Not him. Not until it was time to marry, have children. Why rush things? Life was fine as it was. He had no need for commitment. Not yet.

Not yet, he thought, as Layla laid her hand over his heart.

Not yet, he thought, as he nuzzled her throat.

Not yet, he thought, and rose on his elbow and looked down at her.

"*Habiba.*"

"Yes?"

"My plan," he said slowly. "To keep you from Butrus…"

She nodded. He could see she didn't want to deal with reality just yet, but they had no choice. He captured her hand, kissed the palm and folded her fingers over the kiss.

"You figured out most of it. I'm going to phone my father. Tell him I didn't take you to Kasmir because I wanted you for myself."

She nodded again. "Omar will accept that," she said quietly, "because of who you are."

"Yes. So will Butrus, though I will give him even more reason to do so."

"You'll buy me from him," she said, with a smile that didn't quite reach her eyes.

Khalil kissed her.

"I couldn't do that, *habiba.* There isn't enough gold in the world to equal your worth, yet I will give him enough to silence him." He paused. "But to make all these things work, you must say that you will marry me."

Her eyes met his. "I know. I understand. But…but marriage—"

Again he brushed his lips over hers. Now was the time to tell her the rest of it. That they would not marry. That he would only pretend they intended to wed, then tell his father that he'd changed his mind.

He said none of those things. Instead he drew Layla into his arms.

"Marriage is the only way," he heard himself whisper. "Layla. Say yes."

She took a deep breath.

And said, "Yes."

CHAPTER ELEVEN

WHO was it who said that Paris was made for lovers?

Layla, pessimist that she was when it came to romance, had always figured the saying was the brainchild of some clever marketing guru.

She smiled into the mirror over the vanity as she dressed for the evening. Khalil had been mysterious about it; he'd only said they were going somewhere special, but then, everything in Paris was special.

The marketing guru was right. The city *was* for lovers.

By day it was a stage set of charming bistros and narrow cobblestone streets. At night the city blazed with light. Brightly illuminated boats slipped down the river. The Champs Elysées glittered like a jeweled necklace. And always, day or night, Paris was a place where a man and a woman could look into each other's eyes and forget reality….

If only for a little while.

Layla's smile tilted.

Tomorrow, everything would change. Khalil would phone his father. He would tell him that he was going to marry her. His father would accept his decision, Khalil said. The sultan was not a fool; he'd realize that acceptance was the only way to placate Omar and Butrus. Then he and Layla would fly to Al Ankhara and marry.

She would become Khalil's wife. The wife of a sheikh. A prince. A man who would someday assume the throne.

Layla bit her lip.

Was she ready for that? Better still, was Khalil ready for it? The answer to the first question was an easy yes. She could be ready for anything with him beside her.

He was the kind of man every woman dreamed of finding. Handsome. So handsome that she'd almost grown accustomed to the way other women looked at him. Tall. Dark. Imposing. Imposing enough and commanding enough that men looked at him, too, with something halfway between admiration and resentment etched into their faces.

Always it thrilled her to be with him. To have him curve his arm around her waist, bend his beautiful head so he could speak softly into her ear. *This man is mine,* she wanted to say, *and I am his.*

But it wasn't really true.

He was good to her. Actually, *good* was a pathetic word to describe how he treated her. He was generous and kind, caring and respectful of her every wish.

Her every desire.

In bed… Heat flashed through her blood, just thinking about it.

In bed, Khalil was the most amazing lover a woman could want. She had little basis for comparison—her sexual experience was limited. She'd been with one man, her college boyfriend, and that had only lasted a week before he'd told her he had no time for dealing with a frigid woman.

She wasn't frigid, she'd known that even then, but she

hadn't been very responsive, either. Not enough to experiment again, or even to dream of taking another lover. She knew all the psychological crap that explained it, starting with her mother's fragmented stories about her father when she was very young and ending with the ugly truth when she was, her mother thought, old enough to handle it.

She didn't care. She'd had her studies, her work…

Now she had Khalil. He had changed everything.

Layla closed her eyes as images of their lovemaking suffused her senses.

He was an incredible lover. He was giving; he was demanding. He was tender; he could be excitingly rough. He'd taught her things about sex, about her own sexuality, that made her tremble just at the feel of his hand on her skin.

She wanted him all the time.

It had embarrassed her until he'd whispered that he loved the intensity of her desire, that it only heightened his. And he'd proved it by slipping his hand under the table and beneath her skirt in an elegant restaurant, by pulling her into a shadowed corner of the Louvre and kissing her until she was clinging to him, by bringing her to climax with his clever fingers in the darkened backseat of a taxi as they sped through the city's silent streets.

But there was more. They talked. About politics. About music. About everything and anything. They played games. Chess, where he beat her every time. Poker, where she took all his chips, though she suspected he let her do it. They lay curled in each other's arms in front of the TV, watching game shows so terrible all they could do was laugh.

So, yes, she was ready to become his wife. She knew there would be things that would be difficult to learn about her new role, moments she'd probably have to lean on Khalil's strength, but she could deal with this change in her life.

She would thrive on it.

But could Khalil?

Layla backed away from the mirror and sank onto the edge of the tub.

He cared for her. She knew that he did. And he enjoyed being with her, in bed and out. But—the big, overwhelming, awful but—he came from a world not just foreign to her but alien to her. The customs of his people were not hers. The way in which he lived was not hers. His language was not hers.

Then how could he *be* hers?

He was marrying her because he had no choice. He'd stolen her from Butrus. That was the bottom line. It didn't matter if he'd done it to save his father's honor or to save her life; the end result was still the same.

He had done something his father, her father and Butrus saw as unforgivable, and the only way past that was to exercise his authority as prince and take her as his wife.

It was the logical thing to do.

Was that the way to begin a marriage? Weren't people supposed to have a greater commitment than that? Shouldn't love enter into it? Shouldn't that be the reason for—

"Habiba?"

The light knock on the bathroom door presaged its opening by seconds. There wasn't time to stand up and pin a smile to her lips, but she tried.

"Khalil," she said brightly. "I'm sorry I'm taking so long but I'm almost—"

"Sweetheart." His arms closed around her. "What's wrong?"

"Nothing. Really. Nothing's wrong. I just…I just can't get my hair to stay up the way I—"

He kissed her. Tenderly. Sweetly. Deeply.

"It's perfect," he said huskily. "Those little strands coming loose… They remind me of how you will look later tonight, when we come home and you take your hair down for me and let it tumble over your breasts."

He kissed her again. And, with no warning whatsoever, Layla suddenly understood why she didn't fear becoming Khalil's wife.

She loved him.

She loved him, would always love him, with all her heart.

His Layla was beautiful tonight.

Well, she was always beautiful. Khalil tightened his hand over hers on the gearshift. Tonight she glowed.

She was wearing one of the gowns he'd bought her that first day here, something long, black and slinky. It left one delectable shoulder bare and had a discreet slit up the side that wasn't discreet at all when she sat down and a long length of leg was exposed.

Her shoes were delicate contraptions of straps and glitter, with heels so high he couldn't stop imagining how she'd look later, in those shoes, the silk thong he knew she wore underneath the gown, and nothing else but perfumed skin.

Great, he thought, smothering a groan. There was nothing like turning hard as stone when you were on your way to a posh restaurant.

Layla would love the place he was taking her to, but then, she loved all the places they went.

He smiled to himself as he remembered what had happened yesterday when they'd been strolling along the Champs-Elysées and passed a McDonald's.

She'd stared at the familiar Golden Arches.

"McD's? In Paris?"

She'd turned to him, laughing. He'd wanted to snatch her off her feet and kiss her, but he had the feeling she'd have disapproved, so he settled for flashing her a grin.

"Sure. Want to go in?"

"We have to," she said, sounding solemn despite the glint in her eyes. "I mean, wouldn't it be unpatriotic if we didn't?"

They stepped into a familiar bit of America, though a glance at the menu made clear it really wasn't.

"You order for us," Khalil said. He loved her high school French, the way she furrowed her brow to get the words right.

So she ordered, things half-American and half-French, a McCroque, a Hamburger Royal, "*frites avec* mayo," which made her giggle, a cola for her and a beer for him.

They sat at a small table. Khalil finished eating before she did and reached for one of her fries.

"Hey," she said indignantly.

"*Habiba.* This is a scientific experiment. I'm trying to determine if these are French fries or *frites.*" He took a couple more.

"Liar!"

"Who, me?" he said, slapping a hand over his heart.

She laughed—and he suddenly realized he wasn't just happy, he'd never been happier in his life. Why? How could that have happened? The answer had seemed just within reach. Even now, it still did, if he could only reach out and grasp it...

"Khalil."

Layla's eyes were dark with concern.

"Yes, sweetheart?"

"You look so serious. What are you thinking?"

He brought her hand to his lips. "Only that I hope you like this place, *habiba*. It is, I think, very special."

The restaurant was in the Eiffel Tower, some four hundred feet above the city, tucked in among the steel beams like the nest of an eagle.

The room itself was elegant and spare, candlelit so as not to detract from the blazing brilliance of Paris. The meal was extraordinary. So was their table. It was next to a window. The view, Layla said with unbridled delight, was amazing.

Khalil agreed. His view, however, was of her.

She was far more beautiful than any other woman in the restaurant, more beautiful that any woman he'd ever known. He leaned closer and told her so, and then, because a man could only take so much, he kissed the naked shoulder that had been driving him crazy with desire all evening.

She looked at him, the candlelight burnishing her skin and hair, and he knew it was time.

The enormity of what he was about to do made his heartbeat stumble. He took a steadying breath, reached into his pocket for a small, elegantly wrapped package and placed it in front of her.

She looked at it, then at him. "What is this?"

"Something I hope you will like, *habiba*. Go on. Open it."

Her fingers seemed all thumbs as she undid the ribbon, then the wrapping and finally opened the box.

Her face drained of color.

"Ohmygod, Khalil!"

What did that mean? Did she like the ring? Did she hate it? He'd bought an emerald-cut diamond. Would she have preferred something else?

"Khalil. This is…this is—"

"Don't you like it?" he said, and silently cursed the desperation in his voice. He had given her no choice but to marry him. Still, she'd seemed happy….

"It's the most beautiful thing I've ever seen," she whispered, and when she lifted her eyes to his, he could have sworn they shone like stars.

A joy, so intense it made him light-headed, swept through him.

"Here," he said gruffly, "let me put it on your finger."

The ring fit perfectly. He'd guessed at the size when he bought it yesterday morning, after they'd made love. She'd fallen asleep in his arms and he'd slipped from their bed, dressed hurriedly and rushed off to Cartier's.

He bought and sold stocks by the thousands, dealt in the turnover of corporations whose annual budgets exceeded those of some nations, but nothing had been half as important as purchasing exactly the right ring.

Layla raised her hand near the flame of the candles. All the colors of the rainbow flashed from the diamond's brilliant heart.

"Khalil. This is…it's too much."

Too much? It wasn't enough. She deserved more. She was everything a man could want. She was…she was—

"I know you're a sheikh. And I know that your father and my father and even Butrus must never lose sight of that, but—"

"Do you think that's why I chose this ring, *habiba?*" He reached for her hand, lifted it to his lips and kissed it. "I chose it because it is like you. Beautiful and bright and shining with happiness."

Her smile went straight to his heart.

"Thank you," she said softly. "For saying those things. They…they mean everything to me."

"Layla. I know this isn't how you would have thought to marry. I mean, without romance. I mean, so suddenly, to a man you hardly know. I mean—"

What in hell *did* he mean? He was trying to make her happy. Instead he'd dimmed her smile. "Damn it, I'm making a mess of this. Sweetheart, all I'm trying to say is that we may not have started out as fairy-tale lovers but I will make you happy. I swear it."

He leaned toward her and kissed her, never mind the restaurant was filled with people, and when he raised his head again, the light was back in her eyes.

Their waiter appeared, offering coffee and dessert.

"Do you want coffee and something sweet, *habiba?*" Khalil said softly.

A rush of pink flooded his Layla's cheeks. What she wanted was in her eyes; what he wanted pounded through his blood. Khalil dumped several hundred Euros on the table. He rose to his feet, pulled back her chair, took her hand and led her from the restaurant. He kissed her in the warm Paris night, then drove to the Hotel Georges V.

She hung back as they entered the lobby.

"What are we doing?" she whispered.

"We're going to bed." His voice was rough; he'd almost gone crazy driving here, keeping his hands off her.

"But what will they think? We have no luggage. We don't have a reservation."

"They will think I am the most fortunate man in the world, sweetheart. And we won't need a reservation."

She heard that little touch of arrogance in his voice and knew it for what it really was, the self-assurance of a man who was as good and decent as he was powerful. And she loved it, loved his readiness to take on the world, loved—loved—

"*Bon soir, monsieur, madame,*" a mellifluous voice purred.

"Good evening," Khalil replied.

Moments later, they were in an elevator, being whisked to a luxurious suite. Moments after that, they were in each other's arms.

The next day, Layla at his side, Khalil telephoned his father.

The call began badly but he had expected that. His father was furious. Khalil forced himself to remain silent.

"How could you have done this?" the sultan demanded.

He said that Khalil was disobedient. That he was a disappointment to his people. Then he made the ultimate accusation of all. He said Khalil had dishonored him.

For the first time Khalil interrupted the angry flow of words.

"I cannot deny that I was disobedient. And though it pains me to hear you say it, I understand that I disappointed you. But I have not shamed you or our house, Father."

"You most certainly have," his father snapped. "And, in the process, you have dishonored yourself. You were charged with delivering a woman to her bridegroom. Her father had pledged her to Butrus."

"Her father had sold her. That is the truth and you know it. Sold her to a man we both know to be a brute."

"For peace on the northern border, Khalil. Have you forgotten that?"

"Is that the way decent men negotiate peace?"

His father didn't answer. Khalil knew he had scored his first victory.

"Butrus is a man of no scruples. I will offer him gold. I have no doubt he will accept it—and I will make it clear that he will answer to me if he does not honor the peace he promised."

"You have changed," the sultan said, after a few seconds of silence. "Is the woman responsible for it?"

Khalil looked at Layla. "She is…she is a remarkable woman, father."

"And you want her for your own."

"I do."

His father sighed. "Perhaps you are right. A man's honor is a fragile thing. To have given the woman you love to Butrus would have sullied yours, but you should have discussed this with me."

"With you," Khalil said coolly, "and therefore with Jal."

"Jal has only the best interests of our country in his heart."

"And I do not?"

"I didn't mean that. I meant…" The sultan cleared his throat. "This is not a time to talk about Jal. You must return home and face Omar and Butrus. And the council."

"Will you accept Layla as my wife?"

His father sighed. "I will welcome her as a daughter, my son. And so will all of Al Ankhara."

They left Paris that evening.

Khalil's own plane flew them home. It bore his royal crest. Somehow, that magnified the differences between them. Layla felt a moment of terrifying panic. This could never work, it could never—

"Layla?"

She looked up. Khalil had gone to the cockpit to chat with his pilot and copilot. Now he eased into the seat beside her and took her hand.

"What are you thinking, sweetheart?"

She shook her head, fearing he would detect her uncertainty if she spoke.

"Be honest with me, *habiba*," he said softly. "Tell me, always, what is in your heart and I will tell you what is in mine, *na'am?*"

He was right. That was the only way it could be, between a man and a woman, if their marriage was to work.

"I was thinking— I was trying to imagine myself as…as—" She gave a soft laugh. "What will I be, Khalil? A princess?"

He smiled. "Yes."

"I don't know the first thing about being a princess." She gave another little laugh but he could see the worry in her eyes. "My mother waited tables, remember? I worked my way through college doing the same thing."

He grinned. "Think what a help you will be, supervising the staff when we have state dinners."

She knew he was trying to make her feel better, but it wasn't working. How could it, when so much depended on her acceptance by his father and the council?

"Five minutes with me," she said, "and your father will never believe you took me from Butrus because you wanted me for yourself."

"I told you to speak the truth, *habiba*. Speak it now. Are you really afraid you will disappoint him?" His hand tightened on hers. "Or do you fear the changes marrying me will make in your life? Because your life will change. I can't lie and say that it won't."

"I'm not afraid of disappointing your father," Layla said softly. "I'm afraid of disappointing you. I'd die if that happened, Khalil, because I…I—"

"Because you what, sweetheart?" he said in a husky whisper.

Because I love you, she thought, but how could she tell him such a thing? It would only burden him more.

"I just don't want to make things more difficult for you than they already are."

Khalil curved his hand around the nape of her neck. "Nothing will be difficult, as long as you are beside me."

He drew her to him and kissed her. The kiss began softly. Gently. Then it took fire, and Khalil lifted Layla in his arms and carried her through the plane to his bedroom. They made love, and afterward, when she lay dozing in his arms, that incredible sense of happiness swept through him again.

This time he understood it.

He was in love, deeply in love with the woman he was about to make his wife.

CHAPTER TWELVE

LAYLA stood on the terrace outside her suite in the palace, watching the rays of the afternoon sun dance on the azure sea.

She had been in Al Ankhara for three days. Three days, she thought with a little shake of the head, that had brought home the reality of her new life.

This was not the dream world of Paris, where she and Khalil answered to nothing but their passion. This was her lover's homeland, and despite the way in which he had left it, he was its crown prince, its sheikh...

And she was the woman he had chosen for his wife.

She'd thought she understood that, but it wasn't until Khalil's plane landed on the palace's private airstrip that she'd begun to absorb the full reality.

An honor guard snapped to attention and saluted as Khalil stepped from the plane with her beside him. She could read nothing in the faces of the soldiers, but Khalil had bent his head to hers.

"Acknowledge them, *habiba,*" he'd whispered. "Smile so they know you understand the respect they show you."

Respect? For her?

Khalil had understood her confusion. "You are to be my

bride, sweetheart," he'd told her softly, as he handed her into the back of a limousine. "Everyone will accord you the honor due a princess."

Hassan had met them in the courtyard, his frail body bent almost in half at the sight of his master.

"My lord. It is good to see you again."

"It is good to be back," Khalil had replied. Then he'd taken the old man by the shoulders. "Stand up," he'd said gently, "and greet my bride-to-be. She will be angry with us both if you continue these acrobatics."

The old man had smiled. "Welcome, my lady. I am sure you will bring great joy to my master and to all his people."

By the time they'd reached their rooms—her suite adjoined Khalil's—Layla felt as she had the day they'd gone shopping in Paris. It was Alice in Wonderland time again. How else to explain all this? She'd been a prisoner in Al Ankhara. Now she was its future princess.

It was incredible.

It was wonderful.

It was terrifying, and it was all those things at the same time.

She knew she could come to love this place. She saw it differently now. The palace was a magnificent piece of history, not a prison. The people showed their prince traditional signs of respect, not subjugation. The desert was starkly beautiful, as were the distant mountains. The sea, which had seemed cold and alien the night Khalil had plucked her from it, was now spectacular in its vast beauty.

Still, after three days, things were still unsettled.

She had yet to be presented to the council and to the sultan. Would they accept her? Would they resent Khalil for what he'd done? He kept telling her things would be fine and, God, she hoped they would be…

She wanted everything to be perfect. Not for her sake. For his. She loved Khalil so much…so very much, she thought. If only she could tell him that. But of course she couldn't. He had enough worries without learning he had a lovesick fiancée. Actually, they hadn't spent much time together since they'd arrived.

"Forgive me, *habiba*," he'd said, when he left her the first morning, "but there is much I must do."

She understood.

He had obligations, especially now. He had defied his father and the council of ministers, infuriated Omar and Butrus. There was a lot to deal with.

Omar and Butrus, at least, were taken care of.

She'd had to prod Khalil for information about that, and even then, he hadn't said much.

"I don't want you to think about them anymore, *habiba,* except to know that they will never trouble you again."

It was Hassan who'd supplied the details. The old man had become her friend, perhaps because his aged eyes were able to see deep into her hidden heart. She was sure he knew she loved his prince.

Late this morning he'd shuffled in and gleefully reported that Butrus had retreated to the mountains after swearing fealty to Khalil.

"Just like that?" Layla had said in surprise.

"My master paid him four times your weight in gold, my lady." Hassan's leathery face was creased by a grin. "And warned him of his fate, should he ever cause any sort of trouble again."

"And Omar?"

Another huge grin.

"The last I saw, he was prostrate on the floor at my lord's feet, babbling of his good fortune at becoming the sheikh's father in-law." Hassan cackled. "My lord told him to get up, leave his presence, and not to forget that the palace still has a dungeon." The old man had smiled. "You are very important to the sheikh, my lady."

Very important…but not the woman he loved. Layla sighed as she gazed out at the sea.

She knew she was being greedy.

Wasn't it enough to be very important to a man who'd only asked you to marry him because he had no choice? Khalil enjoyed her company. He was relaxed when he was with her. More than that, he was happy when he was with her. And at night, when he opened the connecting door between their rooms, took her in his arms and to his bed…

Just thinking of what it was like made her pulse quicken.

So, yes, asking for more was greedy…but she couldn't help it, she wanted more, wanted everything. To have him call her beloved, to hear him say "I love you," so that she could say those same words to him.

"Habiba."

Layla swung around. Khalil stepped onto the terrace and came toward her. Her heart lifted.

"Hi. I didn't expect to see you until much later."

He nodded. "I know, but things are moving more quickly than I'd anticipated." He paused; she could see a tension in his face. "The council wishes to meet with you."

Finally. She told herself not to let him see how the prospect frightened her. What if they didn't like her? If they didn't approve?

"Is that good or bad?" she said lightly.

His expression softened, if only a little. "It is good," he said gently. "They are ready to accept you as my bride."

"Oh." She swallowed. "Well, then…"

"And this evening, we will have dinner with my father."

"And that's good, too?"

"It is what is expected."

What was expected, which wasn't the same as "good." She was being greedy again. Wasn't it enough that this time the sultan would be seated at a table with her, instead of watching as she knelt before him with Omar's hand hard on her shoulder?

"Layla." Khalil put his arms around her. "Omar and Butrus are out of our lives forever."

"Hassan told me."

"The old man likes you." He framed her face with his hands, tilted it up to his. "*Habiba.* Be patient. Another few days, this will all be settled."

She smiled, nodded, but then her smile dimmed. "Tell me the truth," she said softly. "They don't want to accept me as your wife, do they? The council. Your father. They don't want to forgive you. They say that I'm not right for Al Ankhara—"

Khalil silenced her with a kiss.

"You're right for me, *habiba.* Now, stop worrying and go and get ready."

He was right. Worrying wouldn't change anything. Perhaps making a good impression on the sultan and his ministers would.

"What shall I wear?"

"Something formal but not too formal. Casual but not too casual. You know."

She didn't, but she'd figure it out. "What are you wearing? A jacket? A suit?"

"A suit." His eyes darkened as he drew her against him. "But first I'm going to be wearing nothing. Nothing but you, *habiba,*" he said thickly.

A moment later they were in his bed.
And the world went away.

The ministers were waiting for them in the council chamber.

The last time she'd been in this room they had talked about her, not to her. She had been all but invisible. Now the men rose to their feet when she entered on Khalil's arm. Each man bowed as he was introduced; each addressed her as "my lady."

The one named Jal, whom she recalled as having been the most coldly outspoken, made the deepest bow. He said he regretted the unfortunate series of events that had brought her here the first time.

But she wasn't stupid; his eyes said something else, a message as clear and hard as a blow to the back of the neck. She was being forced on him and he didn't like it.

Did all these men feel the same way? Would they pretend to accept her because they had no choice? Khalil was their prince. Someday he would be their sultan.

And she would be his wife.

A chill stole into her heart.

Was she kidding herself about feeling comfortable in Al Ankhara? She had already glimpsed the complex inner workings of its political structure. How loyal would a prince's people be to a ruler who had taken a wife from a culture as alien to them as the moon?

"My lady."

Layla blinked. Jal smiled at her.

"I am told you are a student of archaeology."

Was he going to try to build a bridge between them? Had she misjudged him?

"Yes," she said, forcing an answering smile. "I am."

"Ah. Well then, you will appreciate the history of this

room. It dates back to the twelfth century. May I have the privilege of showing you some of its more interesting artifacts?"

She glanced at Khalil. He was deep in conversation with two of the other ministers. Jal, still smiling, made a sweeping gesture toward a cabinet. She wanted to ignore him; he gave her a bad feeling, but Khalil's wife would be expected to know something about diplomacy. Here was a safe chance to practice it.

She smiled politely. "Thank you. I'd like that."

They crossed the silk carpet together, Jal chatting pleasantly about a jade carving, a portrait, an enameled box before eventually pausing before the cabinet.

"Do you see it, my lady?"

Layla looked at the shelves. They held old books and an assortment of small carvings.

"What am I looking at?" she asked pleasantly.

"The future," he said in a low, chilling voice.

She stared at him.

"The prince's future, to be exact. Do as I tell you, if you want him to live."

Say something, she told herself, but she was speechless. Jal's smile was constant; no one looking at them would have thought he was talking to her this way.

"Convince him to stop this foolish game before it goes any further. Do you understand?"

Layla wanted to answer, but her mouth seemed glued shut.

"Listen to me, Miss Addison. If you care for the prince at all, you will advise him to stop this thing before events come to a head and people have to die."

At last, she managed to speak, though her voice shook with emotion.

"Are you crazy," she whispered, "saying these things to me? If I were to tell the prince—"

"But you will not tell him, because if you do, you will be signing both your death warrants."

The room tilted. Layla staggered, put out her hand and grasped the edge of the cabinet.

"His life," Jal hissed, "lies in your hands."

"Layla?" She felt Khalil's arm sweep around her waist. She leaned into him, let his strength support her. "What happened here?" he demanded.

"The lady felt faint, my lord," Jal said, with all the concern in the world. "Perhaps she is not yet accustomed to the heat."

"Layla?"

She looked up at the man she loved. His arm was tight around her, but his eyes were riveted on Jal's.

"Yes," she said, with a shaky smile, "that's exactly what happened. I felt…I felt dizzy, but I'm fine now."

Jal screwed his face into a worried frown. "Perhaps the lady needs some water."

Khalil shot him a contemptuous look. "I know what the lady needs," he growled.

He swung her into his arms and strode from the room. Layla put her head on his shoulder. She could hear the whispered buzz behind them; she suspected that the sight of the prince carrying a woman was not part of Al Ankharan tradition.

Was assassination?

Khalil carried her to his suite, laid her gently on the bed and brought her a glass of iced water.

"You don't have to fuss over me," she said.

He smiled. "I don't, but I want to." His smile faded; his mouth thinned. "Did Jal say something to upset you?"

"No. No, of course not."

"You must tell me if he did, *habiba*. He is a man steeped in the old ways."

"He was showing me some artifacts, that's all. And I suddenly felt woozy."

"It's the heat. He's right about that, sweetheart. You were on the terrace too long a time today."

"I'm fine, Khalil. Really."

"You are more than fine," he said gruffly, reaching for her. *Tell her now,* he thought. *Tell her that you love her.*

Tell him now, she thought. *Tell him that you love him.*

But if she told him now, she might end up blurting out Jal's terrifying threat.

He whispered her name. She sighed his. They went into each other's arms and made love. But afterward, lying in Khalil's embrace, Jal's words returned with terrifying clarity.

She had to do something…but what?

At dusk they showered and dressed. Khalil was heartbreakingly handsome in a dark-blue suit, cream-colored shirt and dark-red tie. Layla wore the silver gown he'd bought her in Paris and the slender silver stilettos.

Hand in hand, they walked through the palace to the sultan's apartment.

The sultan himself greeted them. He was dressed in the uniform of his country, medals glinting against his chest, boots shined to a mirror finish. He was a handsome man, still tall and straight despite his years.

Khalil would look just like him, Layla thought, in another four or five decades.

"Miss Addison." Smiling, he reached for Layla's hand. "Welcome to Al Ankhara."

"Your Highness. It's good to meet you."

"We met before, Layla. May I call you that? I recall it and, I am certain, so do you. But the past is the past. Tonight we start over, do you agree?"

Layla forced thoughts of Jal aside. Tonight she had to concentrate on making a good impression on Khalil's father.

"Absolutely," she said, smiling.

"Good, good. Now, please, what will you have? Some wine? An aperitif?"

The sultan led them out the open French doors to the terrace. As always the setting of the sun had brought with it the coolness of the desert night. Layla was grateful she'd brought along a light cashmere shawl. Khalil wrapped it around her shoulders, then encircled her waist with his arm.

The sultan led the conversation. It was all pleasant and civilized, but Layla's thoughts kept returning to Jal's ugly threats. She also sensed an underlying tension between Khalil and his father.

There was more than a chill in the air tonight, there was a sense of danger.

At dinner, she sat to the sultan's right. She ate as much as she could of each course but worry made it difficult.

The sultan noticed her lack of appetite.

"Is the food not to your liking, my dear?"

"It's delicious, sir. I'm just…I'm not very hungry."

"I was afraid our cuisine might be a bit strange to you."

Roasted lamb and couscous, strange? Was this a test?

"I live in New York," Layla said politely. "I'm used to different kinds of foods."

"Ah, yes. An interesting city. Very modern. Nothing like Al Ankhara."

Layla folded her hands in her lap. "Al Ankhara has its own charm."

The sultan smiled. "One might think you were a student of diplomacy, not of archaeology. That is your field, is it not?"

Layla nodded. "Yes, it is."

"How unfortunate. That you should have put in so much time studying, I mean, now that you will have no use for it."

"I beg your pardon?"

"Our women do not work."

Was he baiting her? Even if he was, how could she let that pass?

"I don't agree, sir. What do you call keeping a home and raising children, if not work?"

"I meant, they do not work outside the home."

"This is the twenty-first century. I'm sure the women of Al Ankhara look forward to full participation in society."

She sat back as a servant cleared the table. The sultan's expression gave nothing away. Neither did Khalil's, who'd been strangely silent during the exchange.

Was he upset by her answers? She couldn't tell. She probably shouldn't have said all those things, but she'd never been any good at lying. Besides, what would it matter, if Jal carried through on his threat? If any harm came to Khalil, her beloved Khalil—

"Habiba?"

She jerked her head up. Khalil had gone from looking disinterested to looking alarmed.

"You turned pale," he said softly. "Are you all right?"

"Yes. Thank you. I'm fine."

Khalil turned to the sultan. "Layla fainted this afternoon, Father."

"I didn't faint!"

Khalil pushed back his chair. "You came close enough," he said firmly. "I think it's best if we make an early night of it."

"Really, Khalil—"

"Really, Layla," he said firmly. "We're not going to discuss this any further."

Layla stared at him. The king of the universe was taking charge again. And yet he seemed oblivious to the important things. Jal's false smiles. His father's none-too-subtle questions. Didn't he see that everyone knew she didn't belong here? She was wrong for him, for his culture, for his responsibilities.

And his life, his *life,* was in her hands.

She took a steadying breath and got to her feet. Both men had risen. Both were looking at her with curiosity. It wasn't easy, but she forced a polite smile.

"I'm sorry, sir. I didn't mean to be rude. I think your son is right. I should get some rest."

"Of course, my dear."

"Thank you for a lovely dinner. No, Khalil, please. I can find my own way. Stay and have coffee with your father."

Khalil came around the table to her. His father turned away. Was he being discreet, or was the sight of his son and heir cupping the face of a woman like her more than he could bear?

"Habiba," Khalil said in a low voice, "I do have to talk with my father but I won't be very long. I'll be up soon." Gently he touched his mouth to hers. "All right?"

Layla nodded. She didn't trust herself to speak.

"Habiba? Is there something you want to tell me?"

Yes, she thought, God, yes. She had to find a way to tell him about Jal…

"Habiba?"

Layla shook her head. "No. Nothing. Except…except," she whispered, "that I—that you—that you are a wonderful man."

He smiled. "Hold on to that thought."

She left him in the dining room, made her way down the hall toward the door through which they'd entered the sultan's quarters…and she realized she'd left her scarf behind.

Layla turned and retraced her steps. She didn't want to intrude on Khalil's conversation with his father; she was sure it was about her. *Everyone's* conversations were about her, she thought, biting back a giddy laugh. But what could she do about it? Khalil had to marry her. Nobody understood that. Nobody knew the truth, that Khalil wasn't marrying her because he wanted her but because—

Raised voices carried to her. She paused outside the dining room.

"…an enormous mistake, Khalil!"

"I am doing what must be done, Father."

"You are flouting tradition."

"Tradition be damned. I am doing what is right."

"It is not right! You are the crown prince. To take such a step—"

"I told you, I have no choice."

"Just answer one question, then. If there were some other way, would you go through with this?"

There was a silence. She heard Khalil sigh. When he finally answered, his voice was low and rough.

"No," he said, "I would not."

Layla stumbled back. Her heart fluttered in her throat.

The voices went on, more quietly now; the two men must have stepped onto the terrace.

She wanted to run. To flee from this place, this terrible place.

Instead, she forced herself to move slowly. Quietly. Down the hall again. Out the apartment door. Across the wide hall, to the stairs.

What a fool she'd been!

She had always known that love had nothing to do with Khalil's proposal of marriage. He had asked her to become his wife because it was necessary.

But she had overlooked one simple truth.

It was the asking, not her acceptance, that mattered.

There was nothing to pack.

That was the good news.

Layla stripped off the Paris gown, kicked off the sandals. She pulled on a silk T-shirt, a pair of jeans, low-heeled sandals and a light jacket.

The bad news was finding a way to leave without causing a stir. She didn't want to embarrass Khalil or cause him any more trouble.

There was notepaper in the desk drawer. She took a sheet, a pen, and started writing.

> *Khalil:*
> *I think we both know this is a mistake. Your offer to marry me…*

No. She crossed that out. She had to make this sound as if leaving was only about her, not about him.

> *Khalil:*
> *I've given this a lot of thought. I can't go through*

with this marriage. I realized tonight that I could
never adapt to your culture. I need freedom. Indepen-
dence. The right to follow my own path. I won't have
any of that, as your wife.

She stared at what she'd written. Would he believe it?
Yes. After tonight's dinnertime conversation, he would.
Besides, he'd want to believe it.

"If there were some other way," his father had asked,
"would you go through with this?"

Layla knew she would hear that low, tortured "no" for
the rest of her life.

"My lady?"

She spun toward the open door that connected her
rooms to Khalil's. Hassan made a deep bow.

"I was preparing the sheikh's room for the night. Forgive
me for intruding. Unless—do you need anything, my lady?"

"No. Nothing… Wait!" Layla hesitated, but what choice
did she have? "I do need something."

"Of course. What do you wish? A pot of tea? Coffee?
It will only take me—"

"Nothing like that." She drew a deep breath. "I need—
I need to fly home. Back to America."

He stared at her as if she'd asked him to help her fly
to the moon.

"My lord is the only one who can help you with that."

"No. He can't. I…I don't want him to know I'm
leaving."

The old man's face whitened. "But you are to marry him!"

"I can't." Her voice shook. "I love him too much to
marry him."

"I do not understand, my lady. If you love him—"

"Hassan. If *you* love him, you will help me. And you will not tell him about any of this."

The seconds dragged by. Then, just when she'd given up hope, Hassan nodded.

"I will do it."

In the end, it was easy.

Hassan led her through the servants' quarters to a van in the kitchen courtyard. She hunched down in the back, among a bunch of empty produce boxes. The guard waved them through; they drove along the same road as before, but this time, they didn't take the turn-off. Instead they drove to the airline terminal.

Layla gave the old man a hug. *"Shukran,"* she whispered. "Thank you."

He nodded. "May God be with you, my lady."

It was late. The terminal was all but deserted. Only a few weary travelers sat slumped in chairs. A porter mopped the floor. The ticket counters were unstaffed. Layla took a seat far from anyone. She looked at the terminal clock, watched it creep through fifteen minutes. Twenty.

How long until a ticket agent came on duty? She didn't care where she went. She'd buy a ticket on the first plane out of… Her breath caught. What ticket? She had no money. No passport. No credit card—

The terminal door flew open. She looked up but she knew who it was even before she saw him; she shot to her feet and raced for the ladies' room.

"As if that would stop me," Khalil roared, as he plowed through the door after her.

She swung around to face him. "Did you read my note?"

"I read it. Try telling me something I'll believe."

"It's the truth. I'm sorry it took me so long to realize—"

"Try again."

His voice was low and furious; his eyes flashed with that same fury. She wasn't surprised. He was not a man who'd ever had a woman walk out on him, but she had to keep him believing her story, had to keep him from seeing that she wanted to throw herself in his arms.

"You have no way of leaving here. Didn't that occur to you?"

"I have money," she lied.

"Really?" His smile was pure silk. "And where did you get it?"

"I…I kept it hidden."

"Where?" His eyes swept over her. "I know every inch of you, *habiba,*" he said, his voice dropping to a husky purr. "Every sweet inch. If you'd hidden something, anything, I'd know."

She felt heat rise in her face. She remembered those moments of hot exploration but remembering changed nothing. She loved him. That was why she had to leave him.

"Sex," she said, trying a different tack, forcing her eyes to stay on his. "That's all it was."

"It would take me less than a minute to prove how wrong you are."

"Damn it, Khalil—"

"Why are you running away?"

"I'm not running, I'm leaving. And I said it all in my note. Didn't you read it? There are too many traditions here. It would be—it would be stifling to live with a man who—a man who—"

"To live with a man who loves you?"

Elation, swift and all-consuming as wildfire, swept through her. Her face lit; Khalil saw it and wanted to shout his joy from the rooftops.

She loved him. She *loved* him. All that nonsense about following her own path through life—it wasn't true. Yes, she had an independent spirit; it was one of the things he adored about her, but she loved him. She wanted him. The truth of it had always been in her sighs, her kisses.

"I love you," he said. "And you love me."

"I don't."

"That's not what Hassan says."

She opened her mouth, then closed it. Anything she said now would be a mistake.

"He says you told him you love me," Khalil said as he walked toward her.

"He's old," Layla said, stepping back. "He's probably confused."

Khalil smiled and kept coming. "He also says you asked him to keep quiet."

Layla stepped back again but there was nowhere to go. There was a sink behind her.

"Well, *habiba?*" Khalil said softly. He wrapped his hands around the rim of the sink, trapping her there. "Did you ask him not to tell me what you had said?"

"What does it matter?" Layla whispered. He was close. Too close. "He broke his promise."

Khalil leaned forward, laid his lips softly on hers.

"You love me," he said. "And I love you."

She wanted to believe him. With all her heart, she wanted to. But it wasn't true.

"No," she said, "you don't."

Khalil nodded as calmly as if she'd just quoted the day's weather report. "And you know this because…?"

"I heard you. You and your father. He said, would you go through with this if there were any other way. And *you* said, no, you wouldn't."

"Absolutely true."

Layla's heart, which had lifted maybe a tenth of an inch, fell back. "See? I was right. You don't—"

Khalil cupped her shoulders. "We were talking about Jal. My father thought I was putting myself in danger if I—"

"You *are* in danger," she said, the words tumbling from her mouth. She grabbed his shirt with both hands. "Jal will kill you if you marry me."

"If I marry you?"

"That's what he told me. He said, if I loved you, I would find a way to convince you to call this off."

Khalil wrapped his arms around her. "Not the wedding," he said softly. "My plan to arrest him."

She shook her head, bewildered. "You're going to arrest Jal?"

"He's been plotting against my father and the throne for a long time. I suspected it but I needed proof. Today one of the ministers came to me with the details of a plot instigated by Jal to seize power." His tone hardened. "Jal is finished, and so are those few who supported him."

"Then…then you're safe? He can't hurt you?"

"Nothing can hurt me, *habiba*," Khalil said softly, "as long as we have each other."

Layla put her arms around him, leaned against him, gave herself a minute of happiness before reality returned. "But I still can't marry you."

"You can. You will. I love you, *habiba*. And I know you love me." He bent his head to hers, brushed his lips against her lips. "Say the words," he whispered. "Let me hear them."

She gazed into her lover's eyes. "I love you. I adore you. But—"

"No buts," Khalil said in that sexy, arrogant tone she'd come to love. "You're going to marry me."

"What about your father? He won't be happy. Those things he said, the things *I* said, tonight at dinner…"

Khalil grinned. "A test. His idea. I had no idea he was going to pull it or I'd have warned you."

"I know. I figured out that it was a test, and I flunked it."

"You passed it, *habiba*. 'Does your fiancée have spirit?' he asked me. 'Does she have the courage of her convictions?' He knows the direction in which I want to lead our people, and he knows, too, that I will need a strong, brave woman at my side." He framed her face with his hands and gave her a slow, sweet, tender kiss. "Layla. Will you be my wife?"

"Yes," Layla said, "yes, yes, yes…"

The door swung open. A woman stepped into the room. Her eyes widened; she slapped her hand to her heart in shock.

"But you are—you are Sheikh Khalil!"

"What I am," Khalil said, "is the luckiest man in the world."

Laughing, he swept Layla into his arms and carried her into the night.

EPILOGUE

THEY were married on the beach at Al Ankhara a month later.

Khalil's two best friends, Salim and Tariq, were his best men.

"There are never two best men," the wedding planner said with an unctuous smile.

"There are now," Khalil replied.

Tariq's wife, Madison, was Layla's matron of honor. The women had met after the sultan announced his son's engagement and became instant friends.

"After all," Madison said, "we're both the brides of the most gorgeous men in the world!"

Not true, Layla thought as she looked at her groom on her wedding day. Tariq was nice looking. So was Salim. But her Khalil was beautiful.

She smiled, remembering how he'd laughed the time she'd told him that. But it was true. He was beautiful and she loved him with all her heart.

Now she was his wife. Tonight he would make love to her for the first time in the past four weeks. Four endless weeks. He wanted, he said, to make love to her on their wedding night as if it were their very first time.

But it always would be like that, she thought as she watched him coming toward her. Khalil would always be her perfect lover. Her heart would always sing at his touch.

"Habiba."

Layla looked up at her husband. What he wanted, what he needed, blazed in his eyes.

"Yes," she said softly.

The one word was enough. A second later she was in his arms, the crowd applauding and cheering as he carried her up the torch-lit beach and into the palace.

Candles and starlight lit their bedroom. Crimson rose petals lay scattered across the duvet. Khalil let his wife slide down his body until her feet touched the floor. He did it slowly, wanting to prolong every minute of this night.

She was so beautiful in her ivory wedding gown. So exquisite. And he hadn't made love to her in what was surely forever.

His eyes never left her as he took off his tie, tossed it away, then undid the top buttons of his shirt. She watched him; he saw her breathing quicken and he went to her, lifted her face to his and kissed her.

"I love you, *habiba,*" he whispered as he stepped behind her.

Carefully he removed the circlet of flowers she wore, took the pins from her hair and let it tumble to her shoulders. Then he undid the row of tiny buttons down the back of her gown.

His arms closed around her; her head fell against his shoulder and he kissed her throat.

Layla leaned back against him, savoring the feel of his embrace. Then she turned in her husband's arms.

"And I love you, my beloved," she said softly.

Khalil kissed his wife, lifted her into his arms and carried her to their bed.

A meeting under the mistletoe

Amy's gift-wrapped cop...
Merry's holiday surprise...
The true **Joy** of the season...

For these three special women,
Christmas will bring unexpected gifts!

Available 5th December 2008

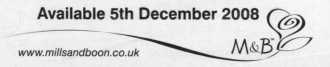

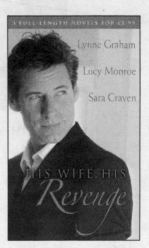

Celebrate 100 years of pure reading pleasure with Mills & Boon®

To mark our centenary, each month we're publishing a special 100th Birthday Edition. These celebratory editions are packed with extra features and include a FREE bonus story.

Plus, you have the chance to enter a fabulous monthly prize draw. See 100th Birthday Edition books for details.

Now that's worth celebrating!

September 2008

Crazy about her Spanish Boss by Rebecca Winters
Includes FREE bonus story
Rafael's Convenient Proposal

November 2008

**The Rancher's Christmas Baby
by Cathy Gillen Thacker**
Includes FREE bonus story *Baby's First Christmas*

December 2008

One Magical Christmas by Carol Marinelli
Includes FREE bonus story *Emergency at Bayside*

Look for Mills & Boon® 100th Birthday Editions at your favourite bookseller or visit
www.millsandboon.co.uk

FREE!

4 Books
and a surprise gift!

We would like to take this opportunity to thank you for reading this Mills & Boon® book by offering you the chance to take FOUR more specially selected titles from the Modern™ series absolutely FREE! We're also making this offer to introduce you to the benefits of the Mills & Boon® Book Club™—

- ★ **FREE home delivery**
- ★ **FREE gifts and competitions**
- ★ **FREE monthly Newsletter**
- ★ **Exclusive Mills & Boon Book Club offers**
- ★ **Books available before they're in the shops**

Accepting these FREE books and gift places you under no obligation to buy, you may cancel at any time, even after receiving your free shipment. Simply complete your details below and return the entire page to the address below. You don't even need a stamp!

YES! Please send me 4 free Modern books and a surprise gift. I understand that unless you hear from me, I will receive 6 superb new titles every month for just £2.99 each, postage and packing free. I am under no obligation to purchase any books and may cancel my subscription at any time. The free books and gift will be mine to keep in any case.

P8ZEF

Ms/Mrs/Miss/Mr ....Initials ....

Surname ....

Address .... **BLOCK CAPITALS PLEASE**

....

....Postcode ....

Send this whole page to:
UK: FREEPOST CN81, Croydon, CR9 3WZ